BEAUTIFUL GAME

Lainey Davis

Beautiful Game

By Lainey Davis

Join my newsletter and never miss a new release!

laineydavis.com

© 2022 Lainey Davis

Many thanks to Nicky Lewis, Melissa Wiesner, Elizabeth Perry, and Yana Ilieva for editorial input.

Thank you for supporting

independent authors!

PROLOGUE: LUCY

"This is Lucy speaking." I almost never answer unknown numbers calling my phone, but I'm on edge today since my ex came to pick up Wyatt. Something seemed off with Nick—more than usual, I mean.

It's bad enough I have to steel my features so Wyatt doesn't see my fear when he has to go with his father for visitation…when Nick decides to show up, that is. But today, Nick was on edge and his eyes looked scary. So, yeah. I pick up the phone for the weird number.

"Lucy…this might seem strange. I've got a little boy here who told me this is your phone number?" The woman on the other end of the line sounds friendly, but concerned. The hair on the back of my neck stands up and I see goosebumps rise on my arms despite the heat.

"Wyatt? Where are you? Who is this calling?"

"My name is Patty Haute. I was out for a run and saw your little guy all alone in the back seat of a car."

"Oh, god! Where are you? I'm on my way."

It's almost 90 degrees outside. I can't imagine why Wyatt would be alone in the car. What is Nick thinking? Usually Nick's antics are aimed at bothering me and making *my* life hard. I'm outside before Patty answers me.

"I just want you to know I called the police and they're on their way here. The doors to the car were all locked with the windows up, so I smashed the passenger window in order to get Wyatt out of the car."

I start sobbing uncontrollably as she speaks. She's so calm! How can I remain calm? "Can I talk to Wyatt? Can I hear his voice?"

"Sure, Lucy. Wyatt? Buddy? Your mom is on the phone." There's a crinkling sound and I hear my little guy babbling something and my entire body exhales. He's okay.

"Mom! This lady broke the window! She did it with a brick! Is she a crook?"

"No, sweetie. She's a hero." My body is shaking now as the adrenaline pulses through me. I'm not sure whether I should drive.

"A hero! Like She-Ra! Do you know He-Man?"

I sit down on the curb next to my car, trying to think. "Can I talk to Miss Patty again?"

"Hi again, Lucy. I'm right here with Wyatt and I can hear the police coming right now. Still no sign of … well, still no sign of whoever's car this is where Wyatt was left alone like that."

"Nick," I mutter. "Wyatt's father. It's his visitation day."

"Ah," Patty says. "You don't need to say any more. Well, hey, we're on the South Side on 22nd Street, just a little back from East Carson. You know, by the bridge?"

"Are you shitting me?" Patty found my kid locked in a hot car along the strip of bars where college students spend their weekends binge drinking. I'm backing out of my parking spot before she can answer, heading away from my apartment toward the party scene where my kid was apparently left unattended so his dad could tie one on with some hot co-eds.

"Hey, Lucy, I'm going to have to go answer questions with these officers, all right? Are you on your way?"

"Yes. I'll be there in ten minutes."

"Don't rush, Lucy. Everything is okay."

She hangs up and I try to rein in my crying while I drive. I don't notice the traffic, am not aware of myself navigating through Pittsburgh's Oakland neighborhood. This is not how I imagined my life would turn out, spending every day wondering what my ex will do to ruin my life. But I can't dwell on that now. I need to think about my four-year-old, how scared he must be.

Maybe that's not true. If he thought Patty was She-Ra he

mustn't be too worked up. I drag my palms down my cheeks as I wait to turn onto the Birmingham Bridge. If I'm going to have to talk to cops, I need to have my wits about me. Usually, Nick manages to twist these incidents so that I look insane. Like he's a stand-up guy and I'm a hysterical, over-protective idiot. The police usually take Nick's side.

I blow out a breath and remember it wasn't me calling the cops this time. Patty is a witness to this. An ally. Maybe this is the day I finally rid myself of Nick. I laugh at the folly of that fantasy. It will never be this easy to get rid of him. But I can't focus on long-term right now.

When I turn onto 22nd Street I see all kinds of flashing lights. A firetruck is there, along with cop cars and an ambulance. I stop my car in the middle of the street and run toward the chaos. When an officer tries to stop me, I can't help but scream. "That's my son over there. Wyatt!!!"

At the sound of his name, he turns from where he's investigating the front of the firetruck and grins at me, waving. "Mom! They gave me a fireman hat! To keep!"

I crumple in the arms of the police officer holding me back, relieved to lay eyes on my unharmed son. I don't really register their questions as the police try to piece together what happened, and soon there are teams of officers entering each bar nearby to look for Nick.

The police won't let me over to Wyatt until I show them my license, and explain repeatedly that I am his mother. It's hard to concentrate as the questions pour in and I laugh maniacally when one of them asks how Nick managed to get partial custody.

One of the firefighters walks Wyatt over toward me and I run over to scoop my son into my arms, covering him with kisses as he squirms to get away from me. "Mom! I was gonna honk the siren!"

The police officer clears his throat and says I have to

answer more questions, and Wyatt seems desperate to get back over to the flashing lights on the fire truck. "It's okay, ma'am," the firefighter says, reaching for Wyatt. "We'll hang on to him for now."

I nod and reluctantly hand him over as I prepare to review my life history with the police officer. Again. How many more times will I have to do this, I wonder, before they stop letting Nick have contact with us? I pull out my phone and search for the email with the current custody order as I explain that Nick actually showed up for his overnight visit for once.

It seems like ages since I left him and used the free lawyer from the women's center to draft this initial custody agreement. I've been scrimping and saving ever since, trying to pay for a new lawyer. I answer the police officer's questions robotically, give him all the information about my address, the name of our case worker with child protective services, all of it.

"I don't have to let Wyatt go with him, right?" A surge of panic pounds through me as I look at the custody order and imagine having to hand my child to Nick after this. The officer sighs and I start shaking my head. "No. No, no, no I won't do it. I'm not going to let him see Wyatt. You can't make me do this!"

He pats me on the arm and tells me he's sorry things have to be this way. "Ma'am, why don't you have a seat? There's going to be some paperwork. Have you heard about an emergency custody order?"

I wipe my nose and try to pull myself together. If I want Wyatt to keep thinking this is a fun experience climbing in a truck, then he can't see me looking a mess. "What do I need to do? For the emergency custody?"

The officer gently places a hand on my arm. "How about you sit on the curb here? I've got a call in for someone to come talk to you, okay?"

I sink to the curb on shaky legs, trying to focus on the deep breathing I use with my clients. Eventually I notice the short-haired woman sitting next to me on the curb. "I'm Patty. Are you Lucy?" She smiles.

I nod, and she does the most amazing thing. She wraps me into a tight hug. "It's all right, Lucy. I'm here and it's going to be all right."

I don't mean to cry into this stranger's shoulder, but I can't seem to control my central nervous system anymore. "Thank you," I repeat as she pats my back and tells me not to worry. I shake and I sob and she just rubs my back until I start to feel like a human. Eventually I look up in time to see my ex being dragged kicking and hollering from a dive bar up the block. He's cuffed and shoved into the back of a patrol car while Wyatt is busy pushing every button on the console of the fire truck. I feel relief knowing he doesn't have to see his father like that.

Patty stays seated next to me as the police officer hands me a stack of paperwork, explaining that I'll need to take it all to family court and file for emergency custody of Wyatt. "I can tell you right now that Nick will spend at least tonight in the county lockup," he says, pointing at the current custody order. "Looks like you have until Wednesday to get that handled before he has visitation again."

Patty places a reassuring hand on my shoulder. "Do you have someone to go with you to help file the paperwork?"

I search my mind, mentally calculate the amount I have in my "get a lawyer" fund. I'm nowhere near the four-figure retainer I need for the lawyer I really want, but I tell myself I can beg her to take payments. I nod to Patty. "I have someone." I take a few shaky breaths and try to extract myself from this kind stranger letting me snot all over her t-shirt. "I'm so sorry," I start to say again, but Patty holds up a hand.

"Hey, none of this is your fault, right? I'm glad I could be here to help Wyatt." I nod, glancing over her shoulder to make sure my son is still occupied with the firefighters. I hear those words all the time since leaving Nick, that none of this is my fault. But I'm the one who fell for him, had a baby with him, stayed with him too long. I brought this all on and I have to figure out how to get past it.

Patty pats my arm. "You've got my number and I've got yours. I'll call you tomorrow and check in." I notice the wet stains from my tears on Patty's t-shirt, which reads *Ask me about my soccer team.* I snort out a laugh. I haven't gotten to play soccer in years, not since before Wyatt. God, I love playing soccer. Loved?

I swallow and gesture at her shirt. "What's up with your soccer team?"

She grins. "Oh! Great question! What do you do on Wednesday nights?"

CHAPTER ONE

Hawk

"Moyer! Boss wants to see you!" My coach's voice snaps into the steamy shower room as I stand with my head against the tile, washing away the grime from practice. I give Coach a thumbs up, too tired to even turn my head and acknowledge him properly.

This is my third season with Salt Lake City's pro soccer team, which means it's my third year as a stand-out player in a mediocre franchise. I've been hoping for this meeting. Coach knows I'm looking to be traded. Last weekend I scored my fourth goal for the season which, if you know anything about soccer, is pretty fucking stellar for a midfielder.

I rinse the shampoo out of my hair, get dressed, and take the elevator up to the manager's office. The big boss. Maybe someday I'll own a pro soccer team like Lou, but then I'd have to put up with cocky assholes like me every day.

I rap on the door frame as I approach Lou's office and hear him grunt from inside. When I open the door, I see my agent, Brian, sitting with his foot up on his opposite knee, his arms crossed behind his head, looking relaxed as fuck. He winks at me as I walk into the room.

The boss looks up from his paperwork. "Ah, Hawk. Have a seat." His voice is flat. I'm sure Lou's irritated that I'm leaving. He can suck my nuts. Everyone knew Utah was just a layover for me. I sink into the chair. Brian leans forward and slaps me on the back.

Lou grumbles and exhales through his nose, folding his hands on top of the papers on his desk. "Well, Mr. Moyer, it appears your tenure with us has come to an end."

I arch a brow and turn to Brian. He grins and squeezes my knee like we're on a date. I look at him. "You landed the deal?" Ever since I went pro, I've been hoping to get traded closer to my mom. I know I could easily move her out wherever I'm playing, but she's stubborn and doesn't want to leave Ohio. Not that I blame her. She's got a real nice support network there with all her church friends.

But Brian knew from the day he signed me that the big goal is to get back to the heart of the nation. I know, I know. Most guys dream of playing in New York or LA or some other glamorous city. What can I say? I'm a mama's boy. It helps that the Midwest has some of the best pro soccer teams in the nation. "Am I going to Columbus?"

Lou grunts and Brian clacks his teeth together. "Not quite. Pittsburgh!"

"Pittsburgh?"

Brian nods. "I checked and it's like the same distance to your mom as Columbus. Three hours by highway, probably less in your speedy little Lambo. Great stadium there by one of the rivers. The Forge were pissing their pants with glee to buy your contract, let me tell you."

"Pittsburgh?"

Lou snorts and Brian waves a hand. "Don't worry about the doping scandal. The players have all tested clean and that coach was fired. It was literally just that one dude messing things up. But Pittsburgh's publicity scandal is why I was able to get you so much fucking money, Hawky!"

I arch a brow at him. I could give two shits about a scandal over performance-enhancing drugs. That is not why I refuse to play for that city. "Do you ever listen to a thing I say?"

Brian holds his hands up. "I do listen, bro. But it's a big city. There's no reason to think you're going to cross paths with your bio dad."

I stand up from the chair so fast it tips over backwards, and I kick it. I stomp over to the window and stare out at the field where I just finished sprinting until I puked. I've worked every second of my life to be great, to distance myself from the shit-stain sperm donor who knocked up my mother and left her to O.D. under a bridge.

I don't even know his name, but I know his entire city is tainted for him being there.

I watched Mom claw her way up from rock bottom and make a life for us, sacrifice so that I always had a way to get to soccer training.

I place my hands against the glass, feeling the cool surface against my palms. "Anywhere but Pittsburgh, man. Come on. I said anywhere but Pittsburgh."

"Pittsburgh had the money, baby. You're going to be getting seven figures, Hawk. Do you know how unheard of that is for a soccer player in the States? You're like elite level hot shit right now." I can hear Lou grumbling as Brian tries to calm me down.

I shake my head. "I'll just stay here in Utah." I press off the glass and turn around to face them again.

Brian slaps me on the back. "No can do, amigo. Trade window closed. Everything is signed. You personally notarized everything and I know you were stone sober when you did it."

I grind my teeth together and turn to stare at Lou, who shrugs. I kick another chair. "I should have played baseball." I start walking toward the door before I really lose my shit. I need to go find a creative outlet for all this rage I'm feeling.

Lou shouts after me as I walk out of his office. "The staff are cleaning out your locker as we speak, Hawk, but I'm sure the team would appreciate a goodbye."

I clomp down the stairs, ignoring the burn in my quads, and when I get to the locker room, there're two security guards holding a box each with my personal crap from my locker. I wonder if they'll even let me keep my duffel bag. It's not like they can do anything with it or pass it on to another player. I peer into one of the boxes and it's just got my deodorant and a picture of me with my mom. I guess they're going to auction my personalized gear for charity. Or burn it.

I thank the guards and take the boxes from them. I'll email the team later. I'm not in the head space to talk to anyone right now. When I get to the parking lot, I pluck out the photo and dump the rest of my shit into a trash bin. I climb inside my car, squeeze the steering wheel, and scream for a few minutes before calling my mom.

Feeling significantly more calm by the time she answers, I greet her in a pleasant tone, noticing my voice is a little scratchy. "Good news, Ma."

"Hey, sweetie. I've asked you not to call me 'Ma' like that. It makes me feel old."

"Ma, you're like 45. That's not old."

"I know, smartypants. I said it makes me *feel* old. Now what's this news of yours? Did you meet someone?"

I groan. I'm barely 26 and she's pressuring me to settle down and get married, as if I'm not a professional athlete focused on my very-demanding career. Except when I'm focused on avoiding the man who slipped me half my DNA, I guess.

I decide to ignore her question and just tell her I've been traded. "I'll be living in Pittsburgh," I tell her, and she squeals. "Brian says I'll be two hours from you."

"Oh, baby, that's amazing! I'll get to see you once a week. Maybe more!"

"You're not driving that far once a week just to see me."

"And who says? I like road trips. I can listen to an audiobook. There's some really spicy ones I've got my eye on."

"Ma, please do not talk to me about spicy books, okay? But if you really want to come I'll have someone drive you or something. I don't like thinking of you alone on the road that much."

"Oh, Hawk, I'm just so excited. You made your mama very happy today. What time is it there? Did you eat yet?"

"I'll eat when I get home. I just got out of practice and found out about the trade. You're my fist call."

There's a pause for a minute and I hear the hesitation in her voice when she says, "I thought you said you'd never play for Pittsburgh…"

I sigh. "I know I said that. Brian also said Pittsburgh offered the most money. He says it's a pretty big city…"

"It is a big city, baby. And I'm glad Brian got you a good contract. You're worth every penny!"

"Thanks, mom."

"There. Was that so hard?" She chuckles. "I think Brian is right. There's no reason for you to avoid an entire city. That's just wasted bad energy, sweetheart."

"Maybe I'd have less rage about it if you'd just tell me who my father is so I can go wring his neck and move on with my life."

"Hawk!" My mother gasps. "You're not being fair. We've been over this so many times…" I was conceived during a very dark time in my mother's life, when she was struggling with addiction and living on the streets. She took up with a man twice her age for protection. "He was in no shape to be anyone's father, baby. I chose to get my act together. You are a gift to me. You changed my life." She always gets emotional talking about it. Like I was the result of a supernatural answered prayer, rather than a drunk slime ball who fucked a teenager.

"He left you to die, Ma."

"Hawk. I made a choice every time I put those drugs into

my body. And then I made a choice to do something about it when I found out I was pregnant. You are the best thing to ever happen to me, and I want to come see you play in Pittsburgh and make new memories there."

I sigh. There's nothing productive I can say right now and I'm too pissed off to keep talking about it. "I gotta go pack," I tell her, firing up my engine with a roar.

"I love you, Hawk. Fly home to me and let's talk more."

I roll my eyes. "Such a cheesy line, Ma." We hang up and I drive   home.

CHAPTER TWO

Lucy

I keep waiting for Patty to tell me to stop calling her before soccer. Almost every week for the past month, I let my nervous energy fly into her reassuring ear, and she just keeps answering the phone. "I feel like such a jerk always bringing Wyatt along." When Patty first told me about the team it sounded too good to be true, the idea of getting out onto a field and running again, moving my legs unrelated to parenting or work.

"I'm one thousand percent positive everyone thinks it's fine, Lucy. Did you ever find your cleats or should I ask the gals if anyone has spares?"

I look down at the tote bag full of snacks for Wyatt, drinks for Wyatt, and my tattered soccer cleats from college. They were in the bottom of a bin in our storage area of the basement, and it's taken me awhile to find the time to search that deeply to find them. I never did find my shin guards, but it's been easy enough to avoid getting kicked.

"I've got my old ones here," I tell Patty. I blow out a breath. Every week, I almost talk myself out of going. At first, Patty had to insist, telling me nobody cared if I'm rusty and out of shape. Only my gratitude for her saving Wyatt compelled me to get in the car.

A few weeks in, and I'm still feeling emotional about the

team existing, welcoming me in when I don't feel like I have anything to contribute. But I know that I'll feel better after I run around, so I tell her, "All right. We're heading up to the field."

Patty introduced me to the Phe-Moms, an over-30 women's soccer team. In truth, most of the women are in their 40s. They joke about being crones, but they play intense, joyful soccer. I had no idea such a thing existed, but honestly, I'm more excited about joining them than I've been about anything since getting approved for financial aid for Wyatt's daycare.

A few times a week, the Phe-Moms get together to play pickup soccer for an hour or so. Just women, mostly moms…playing soccer together. It sounds like some sort of magic club I dreamed up in a fever haze. The concept of all of them carving out space to compete, even for fun, just against one another—it feels like a fairytale. I still marvel that there are really this many moms near me who have their act together enough to exercise as a team.

I find parking near the turf field in Schenley Park and Wyatt scuttles up the hill behind me as I walk toward the field. I exhale a deep sigh of relief when I see a woman there with two little boys. Tawnya, mom to twins Natori and Odongo, has been another divine gift in my life.

"Hey, friends!" Tawnya waves as she holds a child on one hip and then sticks out that arm to prevent another one of her sons from sprinting into the street. He ducks between her legs in a brown blur of curly hair. "Natori had so much fun playing with Wyatt this weekend, didn't you?" She boops his nose and smiles at him before setting him down. He clings to her leg and looks at me curiously.

I smile at her words. She mentioned last week that she was desperate for a babysitter for her twins and I jumped at the chance to help her. It's so rare that I feel like I have anything to offer anyone since my life has been such a train wreck.

Hanging out at Tawnya's house while her twins played with Wyatt was a treat for all of us.

I smile at Natori, and Odongo, who has joined his brother in clinging to his mother's legs. "We had a blast, too. And you really didn't need to order that much pizza for us. I feel like you could have fed an entire soccer team with what you ordered."

Tawnya snorts. "Kioko took it to work with him the next day," she says. "We probably *did* feed the whole team." Our three boys run off to the sidelines together, leaving Tawnya and I behind as we make our way to the field.

I marvel at the comfort with which she takes her eye off her sons, the trust she feels that they will remain safe and intact if she's not staring at them every single second. I told Patty I'm still not over my fear about what happened. I know Nick is on house arrest right now and there's no actual threat to Wyatt, but I can't shake the terror that rolled over me during and, even more, after the events on the South Side. My lawyer advised me not to file any changes in custody until after Nick's criminal proceedings. For now, I have emergency custody since Nick can only leave his house for work. And since he's awaiting trial for endangering our son. My lawyer thinks I'll be able to get sole custody if I bide my time.

I sit next to Tawnya and lace up my cleats while she talks a little about work. Tawnya is the first Black woman to make partner at her law firm and often has events to attend in the evenings. Not on Wednesdays, though. She carves out this night for the Phe-Moms, just like all the rest of the team. Everyone has jobs and drama, they always assure me. But on Wednesday nights for 90 minutes, we all just get to play soccer.

Tawnya and I step onto the turf, passing the ball back and forth. I was delighted the first day I came, when the muscle memory kicked in as soon as my foot made contact with the rubber ball. Then I was so sore the next day I could hardly move. It was a good reminder for me to always make sure I help my clients stretch after our training sessions at the gym.

Patty walks onto the field and hollers for everyone to gather around before we get started. I juggle the ball while she gets organized, just to see if I still can. I grin when I succeed in bouncing it off my thigh, back to my foot. Tawnya smiles and nudges me with her shoulder. "Oooh," she says. "You've got moves!"

Patty looks around the group and says, "You all know we're not getting any younger. Every week, one of you pulls something and we all hear about it." We all laugh. I'm one of the youngest players here. Patty just turned 50 and she's not alone. I feel wistful, hoping I am still playing with them in ten and even twenty years. Patty continues talking. "So I thought I'd put Lucy on the spot and ask her to take us through a warm-up before we get started."

My eyes bulge. "Me?" I hadn't mentioned my work to Patty to brag or take over like this. It just came up when I wore a work shirt to soccer one night.

Patty nods. "I thought maybe you could help make sure we don't tear our groins."

"Or break our ankles!" One of the Heathers rotates her foot and we all cringe at the cracking and popping sounds it makes. Many women on the team in their forties are named either Heather or Jessica, and many of them also have old injuries from their high school or college playing days.

I take a deep breath and look around at their eager faces. I nod. "Okay," I say. "We can do a dynamic warmup." I ask them to line up on the sideline and we skip out to mid-field, walking back. I take them through a few rounds of walking lunges and butt-kicks, feeling ecstatic as the whole team stretches together. They seem truly interested in learning how to safely warm up their bodies. Some of them even ask for ideas to stretch a trouble spot, so I show them some yoga poses for their hips and lower back.

By the time we pick out brightly-colored pinnies to split into two teams, I'm overwhelmed. I've been waiting for a shoe to drop when it comes to soccer and my new friendships. I know better than to hope this will last long. If the past few years have taught me anything, it's that everything good is fleeting. I tell myself to soak it up and appreciate this experience while it lasts. I can enjoy this feeling, of having helped them even in a small way. *It's okay to have fun.*

The game starts and my focus narrows in to the ball, the grass, and the women on my team. My passes aren't as crisp as they were in my early 20s, but I'm playing! I feel an unfamiliar sensation and it takes me a few minutes to realize it's joy. For the next hour, I don't worry about Wyatt. I wave at him during play stoppages, but he's engrossed in talking to his new friends and eventually the heavy weight of worry about him begins to lift.

Today, I'm playing striker and I get to run up near the other team's goal, where my job is to try to score. It takes a long time to get open and find some space, but eventually I receive a pass from our mid-fielder. I plant my right foot, peek up at the goal, and swing through with my left leg, feeling the tingle after my foot connects with the ball. I hear the swish as it lands inside the net and euphoria washes over me.

"God, that felt good," I say, as Patty rushes up to give me a high five.

"Looked good, too," she says. "Way to go."

As we continue playing, I'm reminded of what I liked so much about team sports. It feels good to be challenged in this way and it feels good to be cheered for. It feels good even to make mistakes out here, and have the other people in the red pinnies tell me my efforts were a good idea.

"That's game," Soma, another Phe-Mom, yells, a little after nine. I'm surprised to learn we've been playing for over an hour and I jerk my head toward the sidelines, realizing I haven't laid eyes on Wyatt in a bit.

He and Tawnya's boys are huddled under the bleachers, eating snacks and throwing pinecones. I realize Wyatt has had just as much fun tonight as I have. By the time I left Nick, I was very isolated, so Wyatt doesn't get a lot of time with friends outside of daycare. We didn't really have any friends before now.

Tawnya nudges me with her elbow and points to the kids. "Thick as thieves, right?" I laugh and duck as one of them almost hits me with an acorn.

"Hey," she says. "Want to bring Wyatt to the Forge game Saturday night? I know I'll have an easier time managing Odongo and Natori if they've got a friend along."

"The soccer game?" I haven't been to a professional soccer game since I started dating Nick. I know Wyatt would have a blast. The team was recently promoted in the pro league, but has been under media fire for some sort of doping scandal, and I remember reading that tickets are easy to come by.

I wince. Tickets. "I just don't think that's in my budget for this month."

By the time I set aside money for a retainer for my new custody lawyer, I barely had enough left over for bills this month. I try not to rely on Nick's infrequent support payments unless it's an emergency. I've been saving them in a separate bank account for someday.

Tawnya snaps her fingers. "Lucy, you watched my kids for me at my house for free last week. Even if I didn't get the tickets for free, I'd want to treat you." Tawnya's husband, Kioko, owns the Pittsburgh Forge team. "Let me bring you and Wyatt up into the fancy seats." She looks at me expectantly.

I raise my brows. "Free tickets to professional soccer and an offer to occupy my kid safely nearby?"

"Exactly," Tawnya says. She digs out her phone. "Let me text you VIP parking passes, too."

"Oh, I couldn't ask you to do that."

"You didn't ask," she says, tapping away at her phone. "I offered." She grins and then turns and whistles for her kids. She waves as the three of them march off toward their car.

By Saturday afternoon, Wyatt has told anyone who will listen that his new best friends are taking him to watch soccer. I think everyone in my apartment building has heard this story at least four times.

I'm thankful he's sharing that story and not talking about the incident where his father locked him in a hot car so he could go drinking.

As I'm buckling Wyatt into his car seat, he shouts over my shoulder to tell a person walking their dog, "We're going to watch PROFESSIONAL SOCCER!" I grin and ruffle his hair. As I drive to the stadium, I take another moment to feel gratitude that he's happy. He wasn't traumatized by what happened with his dad.

I'm the only one who was affected by that, and I'm strong enough to handle it. I handled it just like I handle every time Nick calls child protective services to tell another outrageous lie about my parenting.

"I can handle it." I repeat this mantra to myself as I wait in line to enter the VIP lot and flash the e-tickets on my phone to the parking attendant. I grin as he waves me ahead, still marveling at the special treatment and opportunities that have been raining down on us since Patty stumbled across my kid.

Tawnya waves at me from the gate and Wyatt tugs on my arm, wanting to run across the parking lot to his friends. Once we're safely inside the turnstile, I let go of Wyatt's hand so he can follow Natori and Odongo. They seem to know exactly where to go, leading the way as we head inside the stadium's offices.

Tawnya notices me looking around and smiles. "First stop is the media center to wish the team good luck."

My jaw drops. "We're going to meet the players? Woah."

I've worked with high caliber athletes in the past. I don't really get starstruck, since I helped train them and know what sort of work they put in to maintain their levels of fitness. It's been a long time since I was a proper strength coach, though. Plus it definitely feels impressive to get a VIP tour of a pro soccer stadium and full access to the team.

Tawnya pushes open a door and beckons for me to follow as the kids make their way through a line of players waiting for media interviews. Wyatt joins in giving out high fives, eventually coming to a stop in front of two men clad in dark suits.

Tawnya leans in to one of the men, planting a kiss on his cheek. "Babe, this is my friend I was telling you about!" She squeezes his hand and he grins. "Lucy, this is Kioko."

I hold out my hand for a shake and he takes it between both of his, giving me a squeeze. I feel immediately at ease around him, even more so when he bends to greet Wyatt. "And this is the young man my sons have told me so much about, eh? Wait a second. I have something for you." Kioko reaches into a pocket of his suit and extracts a small, black and gold bundle. "If you are going to cheer for my team, you should be wearing their colors, yes?"

Wyatt nods his head like this is the most logical thing he's ever heard. He slowly unfolds a tiny Forge jersey and his eyes light up as he looks at me. Kioko stands back up and looks to the man at his side, who I realize is staring at us intently.

I was so caught up in meeting Tawnya's husband that I failed to notice his companion, looking devastating in a dark suit with his dark hair and dark eyes and dark stubble to match. My breath hitches in my throat when I catch his gaze, but then he grins and winks at my son as Kioko says, "But where are my manners? I almost forgot to introduce my family to the newest member of the Forge. Lucy, Tawnya, boys, meet Hawk. He debuts with us next week."

The man in question nods his head. Kioko thumps him on

the back. "Wyatt, you should probably ask him for his autograph now before he gets too famous and the lines to meet him grow too long!" Kioko laughs as Wyatt's jaw drops.

My son holds out his new jersey and says, "Can I have your autograph?"

I practically swoon as Hawk reaches into his dress shirt pocket for a marker, crouching down to write his name on the yellow lettering of Wyatt's jersey. It's been way too long since I've thought about men. I feel a tingle all over when, in a deep, low voice Hawk asks, "Does your mom want my autograph, too?"

"Yes," Wyatt says, nodding. "Definitely."

"Oh, gosh, that's not necessary," I say, wondering why my voice is suddenly high pitched. Like I said, I don't usually get starstruck. There's just something about a broody man who can turn on the charm when it comes to young kids. Okay, this specific man. God, he's hot. Obviously this professional athlete is just being polite while his boss is standing nearby.

Hawk looks up at me. "Oh, I think it's definitely necessary." Glancing at Wyatt as he reaches in his shirt pocket again, Hawk asks, "What's your mom's name, bud? Lucy, was it?"

Wyatt nods. Hawk extracts the stub of a parking garage ticket and starts to scribble on it. Kioko looks at his watch. "My apologies, but we have to get going." He gestures his head toward the hall behind him.

Hawk hands me the parking ticket, letting his fingers brush along mine. I look up and the man winks at me. He winks!

Once they're gone and the twins are helping Wyatt into his jersey, Tawnya starts to fan herself. "Lucy Nelson! The heat between you two was insane. Let me see what he wrote."

I'm about to tell her she's being ridiculous, when I see the autograph. *Lucy, thanks for being my number one fan.*

Tawnya starts screeching with laughter. "He likes you! This is amazing. We have to text the Phe-Moms. You should give him your number."

I shake my head a few times, trying to process.

"He's hot, right? I'm not just old and married?"

I look at her incredulously. "Hot doesn't begin to describe him."

Tawnya hugs me and then whistles for the kids. "Oy! Boys! Let's go find our seats!"

CHAPTER THREE

Lucy

"I don't understand why he's sitting up in the box with us," I hiss at Tawnya, trying not to look back at Hawk sitting beside Kioko in the owner's box. Even though Hawk and Kioko are up in the second level of seats, I feel like Hawk's sitting right behind me, peering into my soul.

She just shrugs and gestures at the field. "He probably hasn't officially started yet or something. Honestly, you should go back and sit next to him and ask him that question." She starts to elbow me until I squirm away from her and she cackles. It's hard to concentrate on the game knowing Hawk is so close by. He's so...smoldering. I'm sure he was just teasing with the autograph business, but I'd be a big liar if I pretended my mind isn't drifting off into fantasyland about the possibilities there.

I might actually be his number one fan already. I laugh off the idea. I sometimes forget that I'm allowed to fantasize about men if I want to. Nobody's going to scream at me for doing so. Remembering this makes me want to sit and imagine Hawk with no shirt on, just because I can, damn it. Obviously I'm not in a place in my life to pursue any sort of anything with anyone. But looking is just fine.

Looking is fine, I repeat before I glance over at Wyatt and grin. He and the twins are pointing at all the players and talking about which ones have good haircuts. They have no consensus on what constitutes a good haircut.

Tawnya elbows me again while the team captains are doing the coin toss before the match. "Lucy. Hawk-the-hottie is sitting right behind us. Ask him about moving here." She is definitely not hitting a good balance between whispering and being heard above the stadium music.

I blush. "Pass"

Her eyes bug out, like she's trying not to explode. "You should offer to give him a tour of the city." I roll my eyes at her. "I'm serious," she hisses. "No strings sexy times with a professional athlete who's into you?"

I pat her hand. "I don't need to tell you that my life is a shit show right now. But I appreciate your support of my fantasies."

She rolls her eyes right back at me. "Oh, come on. The fact that your life is a shit show is exactly why you *need* to get plowed by a super fit athlete who isn't interested in anything past that." She turns around to face her husband. "Hey, Keeks, can you get us some soft pretzels? And some beer? None of the cheap stuff." He gives her a thumbs up and she turns back to face me.

But I won't turn around to look at Hawk. I will not. I keep my eyes on the field, where the players are taking their positions and jumping up and down to shake out the nerves before the kick-off. I miss that feeling. That moment in time before the kick-off was the most stressful part of the game—the anticipation, the not knowing. Once everyone is in motion, the nerves melt away for me.

A memory of my ex flaring his nostrils sneaks into my consciousness, and I remember feeling that same anticipation. Only it was mixed with terror. I didn't know what he was going to do, but in the end I learned the wide range of what that could look like. The stakes were a lot higher than just wondering if the opposition would go right, left, or charge the center of the field.

I squeeze my hands into fists and release them, trying to shake the bad memories. But Tawnya notices. Her face turns from happiness into concern. "What's up, Lucy?"

I wave a hand. I don't know whether Patty told the team anything about Nick's actions before I met the Phe-Moms, but I definitely don't want to talk about it here where both my kid and Hawk can hear. On the field, the Forge steal the ball and charge up the pitch toward their goal. The energy in the stadium turns wild as the fans cheer on the team. I join in, and then groan along with them when Charlotte recovers the ball.

"Oh man," I moan. "That would have been a perfect drive ball. Where was the support?"

Kioko clucks his tongue, leaning in to hand Tawnya the food. He's got a strange expression on his face as he considers me. "You are not wrong! We are just not fast enough," he says. "Mmm mmm mm we have *got* to find a replacement for that drug fiend fitness coach. Firing him left a huge hole in our staff."

Hawk makes a grunting sound of agreement from behind me and my heart leaps a little in my chest. But then the Forge get the ball back and take a shot at the goal and the sound of the crowd distracts me from focusing any more on their conversation.

Through most of the second half, I feel the burn of Hawk's eyes on the back of my neck. A few times, when I turned in my seat to grab a beer or check on the kids, he actually winks at me. Slow, deliberate winks like he fucking knows he is being sexy. After the third such display, Tawnya grabs my arm and drags me to the back of the executive box, where there's a doorway into the club offices.

"Lucy," she hisses. "You have to go out with him. Do it for all of us who are well past such opportunities." She holds her hand over her heart and looks to the heavens.

I snort out a laugh. "It's a lovely idea, Tawnya. But I'm

going to have to remind you about the four year old boy currently high on cotton candy fumes, sitting out there with your kids."

Tawnya cackles. "Don't you dare use Wyatt as an excuse. I will take that child into my giant SUV and tuck him into bed between my kids and sit up all night waiting to hear the recap of your misadventures."

I make a face at her. "Yeah, yeah." I look at my reflection in the glass door and fluff my hair a little bit, straightening my shirt. In another lifetime, I imagined being the kind of mom whose kid had sleepovers. It's been such a project disentangling myself from Nick that I've never actually managed to get a night away from Wyatt.

"Lucy, I'm serious. Kioko and I are happy to have Wyatt sleep over. Have you seen him with our boys? They're best friends now. They told me."

I bite my lip. "The boys do seem to get along." The three of them crawl up the steps toward us and then back down again, making animal noises. I love that Tawnya brought us somewhere they can run around and be noisy. What would it even be like to get a quiet night all to myself?

Tawnya squeezes my shoulder. "Oh my gosh, I want to do this for you. I want you to have a night that's just for you! Please let us take Wyatt overnight? He can share the boys' clothes and we've got toothbrushes to spare."

Wyatt must have heard the word "overnight" because he whips his head around and squeezes one of the twins' arms. "Am I gonna have a sleepover? A slumber party?" His eyes are as round as soccer balls and the twins start babbling about how they love sleepovers with their cousins.

Tawnya drapes an arm around my shoulders and nods at Wyatt. "Your mom is just about to say yes and let you come home with us, bud! I'll even make pancakes in the morning."

I sigh and nod and Wyatt and the boys squeal. "Mmm," I say, leaning back against the wall of the box. "This is going to be weird, though. Not worrying about him."

"Gee," Tawnya taps her chin. "What could you do with that spare energy and free time? Perhaps give the new soccer star a tour of our fine city…"

I roll my eyes at her. "I don't even know if he's into me. I haven't been with anyone in years, Tawnya, *years*. And the last guy was my ex." I groan. "I also don't just go up to guys and ask them out. This isn't…me."

Now she crosses her arms over her chest and arches a brow at me. "Do you actually not want to even go out with him or is this about something else? Because I'm here to listen, while also gently encouraging you to hop on that joystick."

I puff out a laugh. "What would he see in me? I haven't exactly been taking care of myself the past few years." I drop my voice to a whisper and take a quick peek down the stairs to verify that the men are still sitting near the front of the box.

Tawnya pats my arm. "The thing I know about professional athletes is that they don't bother to hit on women they're not interested in. Who better to try something casual with? I think you need this. And I think it'll be fun."

I sigh and start walking back to our seats. As we walk past Kioko, I hear him explaining to Hawk that the players will be hosting the opposition in the club bar after the match. I can't help myself and I blurt out, "doesn't your team nutritionist have thoughts about that idea?"

Hawk raises a brow and Kioko frowns. "Nutritionist?"

My eyes bulge out of my head. "Your team doesn't have a nutritionist? Who makes the diet plans for the team?"

Kioko shakes his head and holds out his hands. "You see? This is what I am talking about. We need to replace that good-for-nothing pirate." He looks at me hopefully. "You know about such things?"

"Well, I'm not a nutritionist. But—" There's a roar of celebration in the stands as the Forge sink a shot into the right corner of the net. Pittsburgh is up by two with minutes remaining. I smile, watching the team celebrate.

Then I feel a shiver as Hawk stands, leaning in close to talk to me. "You gonna stay for a drink, Lucy, to tell me what it is that you *are*?"

CHAPTER FOUR
Hawk

At first I worry that Lucy won't come along to the bar. Not that it would be so hard to find a woman down to fuck…but I don't want another woman. She caught my eye, Lucy with no wedding ring. I watch her whisper furiously with Tawnya and then stoop to kiss her kid goodnight. And then I grin because she turns to me shyly, tucking her hair behind her ears. She's definitely interested.

I nod my head toward the door. "Join me?"

She bites her luscious bottom lip and hesitates. "The team won't even be there yet."

"Good," I tell her, with a half-smile playing on my lips. "I won't have to share you with anyone." I step into the elevator and raise my brows, expectantly, and I grin when she steps inside with me, leaning against the wall, studying me. I loosen my tie, knowing she likes what she sees.

We both step out on the ground floor and make our way into the club house, where a few members of the medical staff from both teams are sitting around one of the tables with a pitcher of beer and some plastic cups. "What's your poison?" I don't really know or care if there's restrictions on what players can order.

Lucy ponders the question, tapping a finger against the bar. Her nails are short, unpainted. She's a low-fuss woman, wearing cut-offs and a t-shirt. I like that. "It's been a long time since I drank," she admits, scrunching up her face. "I guess just a light beer?"

I nod and reach into a bucket sitting out on the bar, grabbing two bottles. I twist off the caps and hand one to her and grin. "What should we toast?"

She smiles. "To Pittsburgh," she says. "The iron city."

I lean closer to her, my mouth an inch from her ear. "I can think of a few things that are made of iron." I don't miss the quick shift of her eyes, glancing down my body. "Barbells," I say, inching closer still. "Bridges...the thighs of a midfielder..."

Lucy laughs. "That was terrible."

"You think I'm joking, Lucy?" I trace a finger through her hair where a piece is stuck to her collar bone, watching her shiver beneath my touch. She looks up at me, pupils blown, chest heaving. She's into me, and I'm into that. "Should we get out of here?" *Too much.* A hint of uncertainty flashes over her face, so I say, "We could check out the field. I haven't even felt the turf here yet."

She grins and sets her beer on the bar. "I'd love that, actually."

"Well, come on, then." I grab her hand and tug her through the bar as the final fans make their way out of the stadium. It's much quieter out here now that everyone's gone, except for a few random groundskeepers. There's a fence separating the bleachers from the grass but I hop over it easily. I turn to hoist Lucy over the fence but see she's got a sneakered foot pressed into the wire mesh and is mid-swing heaving herself over. I smile and nod slowly. This woman is all sorts of surprising.

She inhales and looks up into the stadium lights and sighs. "This is amazing. Look how flat it is."

I love being on the field alone. I often come early on game day just so I get a chance to walk up and down the sideline, getting a feel for the turf that day. Depending on the weather, it can be a totally different experience from one week to the next. I spy a ball off to the side and walk toward it, toeing it back. I drape my suit coat over the fence and gently tap the ball in between my feet. "Yeah," I say. "This is a good field."

"I love how the breeze from the river comes through here. Makes it so much cooler." Lucy seems like she's just wandering toward me to make conversation, but before I can react, she swipes the ball from me with her foot, scooting around behind me and dribbling her way toward the goal.

"Oh, hell, no," I say, immediately sprinting after her. She laughs as she weaves around with the ball. Lucy is no newbie. I get in front of her, blocking her way to the goal and in a few moves, manage to get the ball back, charging away from her.

She's on me in a flash, close up in my space, faking me out as she darts out a foot to steal the ball. "Bet you can't score," she says, her face lit up with joy as she succeeds in snatching the ball.

"What do I get if I do?" I check her with my hip and spin behind her, easily scooping up the ball, even in dress shoes, bouncing it from my knee to my shin, showing off now as I try to circle her.

"Well," Lucy says, biting that lip of hers and stealing the ball back with her knee. "What do you want?"

"I want everything," I say, maneuvering into her space and then jogging backwards, toeing the ball along with me when she tries to steal it again. "But how about a kiss?" I look up at the goal. I'm pretty far back to make a shot, but I'm a professional and I'm confident.

She laughs. "I guess that sounds fair. But you're not going to score." She gets low, like she's ready to block a kick. I fake right, plant and swing and she pivots an instant too late. The ball sails into the net and I step right in front of her, both of us breathing heavy.

"Ready to pay up, Lucy?"

She shrugs. Her eyes dance in the lights from the bleachers and then we're plunged into darkness as the grounds crew shuts them off. She gasps at the sudden sound and I wrap an arm around her waist. "You all right?" My mouth is close to her ear. "Cause I'm about to rock your world with this kiss."

I feel her relax as she laughs and swats at my chest. "Cocky," she says.

I shake my head. "It's not cocky if I can back it up."

She draws in a breath and tilts her head back, parting her lips. I lean in and press my mouth against hers. I intend to be gentle, but she wraps her arms around my neck and pulls me close. I moan in surprise and feel her lean into me. Lucy kisses me fiercely, her tongue swiping across the seam of my lips, her hands smoothing along my chest.

I slide my tongue into her mouth and feel her open to me, yielding. She moans as her hips grind against mine and I wish I'd taken her into an office or something instead of out here on the field, in the open. Because I cannot get enough.

But then she pulls back, breathless. She gathers her hair in one hand and tugs it back over her shoulder, panting. "I have to go," she says, her eyes searching in the darkness, looking for the exit.

I nod and walk with her toward the fence. "You need help ov—okay, nope." I laugh as she hops the fence again with ease and I follow her over. "You gonna call me sometime, Lucy?"

She reaches the exit and turns over her shoulder. She grins. "Maybe." And then she's gone into the parking lot before I can give her my number.

CHAPTER FIVE

Lucy

"That's game!" Once again, Soma is keeping time for us. She jogs over to the sideline and turns off the speaker blasting tunes as the Phe-Moms wrap up another session of pickup soccer. I take a minute to catch my breath before stripping off my neon pinny and looking for Wyatt.

I grin when I see him under the bleachers by the turf, trading cards with Tawnya's boys. I'm still proud that I agreed to let him sleep over at a friend's house. And...I had a *moment* with Hawk. I almost got carried away with him, lost in the sensation and the newness of kissing him, flirting with him on the field. It felt so god-damned good to let go of my inhibitions, to have fun. Like I could be carefree for a minute.

Of course, I feel carefree each time I come to play with the Phe-Moms, too. I'm sleeping better since I started soccer, and I'm in a better mood at work. Each time I kick the ball or sprint as hard as I can, I imagine my body cleansing itself of one more terrifying memory. But those memories are exactly why I had to put a stop to things with Hawk before they got too far. I'm still too messed up to fully let my guard down with a man. No matter how tingly I feel when I touch him.

Soma smiles over at the kids and says, "It's good for the little ones to see their moms claiming this time, moving our bodies, pushing ourselves. Don't you think?"

And I nod, because I do think that.

"You staying for a drink?" Tawnya tilts a can of beer in my direction and wags her eyebrows. I bite my lip, considering. It's after nine, but it's not like Wyatt is going to fall asleep the second we get home anyway. "Come on," she says, handing me the drink. "The boys are deep in a Pokemon discussion."

I doubt my four year old knows the real rules of Pokemon or how to play the actual game, but he seems pretty content looking at the pictures on the cards with his friends. I shrug and crack open the beer, sinking to the turf with my team.

"How was the game last weekend?" Patty clinks cans with me and sits beside me to stretch.

At this question, Tawnya's eyes light up and she claps her hands. "Yes, Lucy, why don't you tell us how *the game* was?"

I glare at Tawnya and whip my head back to Patty. "Honestly, it was amazing. VIP seats. Other kids for my kid to hang out with. Terrific atmosphere."

The night was perfection even without the hot kiss. It's been years since I went to a sporting event. I miss that. When I was pregnant with Wyatt, Nick convinced me to leave my dream job training the men and women's soccer teams at Pittsburgh University. I groan just thinking about it now…how much I let him manipulate and isolate me. He made my life a living hell for so long…I resent the lingering effects he's had on my self esteem, too.

But that all feels too heavy to share with my new-found soccer friends. And I'm not ready to talk about the kiss. Although that was really the icing on a magical evening. I sip my beer, hoping the team will change the subject. They do.

Soma frowns into her beer and says, "I wish the media would give the Forge a break. Honestly, I'm kind of tired of reading about the drama stuff." There's a general murmuring of agreement from the other Phe-Moms. Soma shrugs. "It is shitty timing, though. That the fitness coach guy was caught trying to sneak steroids into the players so soon after they got promoted in the league."

One of the Heathers tilts her head to the side in confusion. "How do you sneak drugs into someone anyway?"

I perk up at this question. "Oh, there's lots of ways people cheat. Some professional athletes get infusions of oxygenated blood before performance. So it's not necessarily even a drug, but it's doping."

They look at me in horror and shudder. "That's fucked up," Soma says. The conversation pivots quickly, and eventually people start wandering off for the night.

Tawnya and I head over to the bleachers to extract our kids. Wyatt starts to cry, and I can tell he's really tired. "Come on, bud. You'll see your friends soon."

"I want to sleep at their house! I hate our house."

Tawnya grins. "We'll have you over for another sleepover soon. I promise!" She winks at me and I blush. After I left the stadium, the experience of a night alone in my bed without worrying about my son was overwhelming. I slept so hard I didn't even dream.

But all the nights since? Oh, yeah. I dreamed about Hawk. Holy shit, have I been dreaming about Hawk. I forgot how good it feels to feel good. Even just fooling around with him and a soccer ball felt good and that was before he put his mouth on mine.

I shake my head. "I hate imposing on you like that, T. I wish I could have all three of the guys over to my place. I just don't have anywhere to put them all…"

I drift off as she waves a hand at me before picking up a kid in each strong arm. "Please. When are you going to believe me that more kids is like fewer kids? They keep each other busy and Kioko and I can relax! Having Wyatt over would be doing us a favor."

"I just don't see it," I say, as Wyatt pulls on my hair and

tries to drink from my water bottle peeking out from the top of my bag.

She laughs. "That's because you only have one." We walk down the hill from the turf to find our cars. Tawnya gets both her boys buckled into their car seats before I finish wrestling Wyatt into his. I keep trying not to compare myself to the other moms, who all seem so much more capable. Tawnya keeps reminding me she gets a lot more down time to restore her energy than I do, and she has an entire other adult at her house to help answer the endless kid questions.

"Oh, hey," she pauses and turns back to me. "Kioko asked me to follow up with you. He was curious since you mentioned the drive pass and the nutrition thing at the game, and then apparently your name came up when he was hanging out with the head soccer coach from Pittsburgh University."

My eyebrows shoot up. "Doug mentioned my name?"

Tawnya waves a hand. "We were all having dinner and I was talking about Phe-Moms and how you get us warmed up before practice so we don't tear our groins. Doug spoke very highly of you! You never talk much about yourself...I had no idea you used to work with him."

I curl my lips in. I don't like to brag about myself. It feels conceited or something. Didn't I give Hawk shit for being cocky? Nope, can't think about Hawk. "Well, it was a long time ago."

She squints at me. "Kioko is desperate for a new coach. You heard him say that. He asked me if it's okay for him to call you."

I blush and hand Wyatt a packet of crackers. He looks up at me from his car seat. I give Tawnya the quick run-down of my degree in kinesiology and my stint as the strength and conditioning coach with the university. Tawnya squeezes my arm. "I'm going to stop you right there. You need to tell all this to Kioko. I'm calling him."

I shake my head. "No, seriously, Tawnya, I just work in the

gym in Bakery Square now. I didn't mean to butt in with Kioko about the guys getting a beer after the match."

Tawnya slices a hand through the air. "Not at all. Kioko is trying to get things right. He's under intense media scrutiny since the whole doping thing." I nod, remembering the news clips on the TVs in the gym today. The reporter was talking about the team interviewing Kioko...then I had to force myself to look away and concentrate on my client when they showed clips of Hawk giving a media interview before practice.

"I really don't think Kioko wants someone like me on his staff..."

She shakes her head as she rummages in her pocket for her phone. "You have training in this field? Certifications and stuff?"

"Well, yeah, but..."

She cocks a dark brow at me. "But...you think a penis is required to coach a men's team?"

I shake my head feebly but she's already dialing her phone. "Keeks. You're going to be so excited to bang me later. I'm about to solve all your problems." I hear a loud laugh come through her phone. She continues, "Yeah. Lucy *is* a strength and conditioning professional. Certifications, experience, the works... Mmm hmm...I know! ... She says it's okay to call her." I glower and Tawnya sticks her tongue out at me. She smiles into the phone. "Yep, see you in an hour."

She points the phone at me. "You've got a job interview. He's gonna text you." Before I can argue with her, tell her she's done too much for me already, she's skipped off to her car and squealed away. She opens her window and sticks an arm out to wave as she tears off down the road like she didn't just offer to change my life.

I check to make sure Wyatt is still buckled and when I close his car door, I rest my head on the roof of the car for a minute, catching my breath. Tawnya's news has thrown me through a real loop. Kioko was talking about me with Doug, my former boss…in a positive light. I had long since given up hope of returning to the collegiate level of coaching, and now I have a job interview with a professional team?

I climb in the car, trying to decide what to do. I think about the lawyer's fees, and what a difference it's already made having someone competent in my court. I'm competent when it comes to strength training and team fitness…plus the money's sure to be good. I peek at my son in the rear view mirror as he tugs on the velcro straps on his shoes. "You ready to head home?" He nods and I start driving, imagining how I'll respond when Kioko calls. Wyatt falls asleep within a few blocks of the field, and my phone dings with the incoming text message Tawnya told me to expect.

CHAPTER SIX
Hawk

My mom calls before eight in the morning. I groan, not sure I like being in the same time zone as her. "Ma, it's early," I say, listening to her laugh.

"I just wanted to hear how things are going. Did you do a good job in practice?" I try not to think about this week's sessions so far. It was my first time really meeting the team and I didn't exactly make a great showing.

"I'm still finding my way," I admit, letting my voice drift off.

"Oh, honey pie, I know it's hard to meet new people and new routines and stuff." She tries to soothe me from afar and I feel bad complaining to her. Here I am dripping with money and opportunity, complaining to my mom that my week as a professional athlete on a new team was less than glamorous.

"It'll be fine," I tell her. "It's the same game everywhere, right?"

"That's right, Hawk. Today will be a better day. When do you have to leave?"

I pull the phone away from my ear and look at the time. "Um, now...we have a press conference this morning."

"Press conference! Look at my boy. Talking to the media."

"That's nothing new, Ma."

She laughs. "I guess not for you. But now you're close by

enough that I might actually see you in our paper."

"You don't think they prefer to run news about the Ohio teams?"

"I'm allowed to be excited for my baby," she chides. "Let your mother gush."

I sigh and get up, tugging on some Forge sweats and the new sneakers my agent sent over. "You can gush, Ma. I love you."

"I love you, too, baby. Talk to you soon?"

"Looking forward to it."

"I'm happy to take your questions." Kioko spreads his hands wide, addressing the members of the media throughout the room. He asked me to join in on the press conference in case people had questions for me, but I can tell the majority of the action is for him, for the coach, and for our team captain. They've all repeatedly assured everyone that no current members of the Forge engaged in illegal doping, but the smell of scandal is too tempting.

I zone out as the reporters ask more questions about the dangling forbidden fruit of high-tech illegal drugs, and whether the team thinks that's a sound strategy for their first season in the premier league. I actually don't know how the former trainer got caught, but he certainly didn't go out quietly. I've only been in town for a week, but I feel like I've heard a month's worth of complaints about how that guy screwed everyone over.

The reporters ask all the usual questions about how we're preparing for the game, how Kioko plans to maintain our fitness regimen with the coaching vacancy…honestly, I tune out.

My mind drifts back to Lucy, how she wasn't afraid to play soccer against me. How she kissed me. Like a fool, I've been checking my phone all week to see if she reached out. I did give her my number with my autograph, after all, but she never gave me hers. I have no idea what I'm doing with this whole scenario. I've picked up beautiful women before. Hell, I know what I look like and I know the work I put into my body. I've seen beautiful women in all stages of undress. It wasn't her beauty that froze me in my tracks. There was just something magnetic about her, like she had some sort of ferocity forcefield around her. She emits this sense that she can do anything she sets her mind to. I'm sure if I played against her long enough, she'd score on me in a soccer match. There's really nothing hotter than a woman who's good at soccer.

I want her to set her mind on me, damn it. I realize I'm nodding along with these dirty thoughts when Kioko turns to me and says, "I'm glad you agree, Mr. Moyer." He nods his head in my direction and I shake myself to attention. "Hawk here is going to revitalize the midfield. He's a deceptive runner, an electric player. I promise, you are all in for a thrill. He makes the beautiful game all that much more beautiful."

I smile, admiring how Kioko invokes the international nickname for soccer. "Hawk, will you be starting this weekend against Baltimore?" A reporter from the front row stands up and holds his little recorder in my direction.

I shake my head. "Hopefully I'm able to elevate my performance this week at practice and earn a starting spot."

I say a quick prayer of thanks for all the media training I did with my college team. I can answer these questions with my eyes shut if I need to. Always flip back to the team, team effort, great coaching, the heart of the opposing team. Yada yada.

It helps that I'm not known for being an attention whore with the media. I know my stats. But I also am well aware that there's ten other guys on the field making it possible for me to achieve anything out there.

If only I had the same autopilot mode when it comes to mentions of this city, why I don't want to be here, and oh yeah. My biological origins.

All I can ever think of are the evenings when my mom didn't know I was still awake, listening to her cry quietly in her bedroom while she tried to map out the bills, wondering how many extra shifts she'd have to pick up at Grocer Joe's to cover the gaps.

I squeeze a water bottle in my fist while the press keeps asking questions. Eventually I look up and Kioko is gesturing at me like I missed a question.

"Sorry," I mutter. "I'm a little jet lagged. Can you repeat the question?"

"Yeah." An irritated-looking guy in a houndstooth blazer seems like he's going to trash me in print. "I asked what excites you most about being here in the Steel City. You've got family in Loudonville, Ohio?"

I nod my head. "That's right. My mother is south of Cleveland. It's great to be in the same time zone."

The reporter looks at me funny, like maybe I missed half the question or said something odd. I quickly add "plus, you know, I was actually born in the 'Burgh. So joining the Forge is a true homecoming."

The reporter looks at me strangely and I turn to face Kioko, wondering where I went wrong. Kioko clears his throat and leans into the mic. "I'm sure you can all appreciate that the team is eager to get to training. We have a big weekend ahead of us. That will be all for today."

Coach Todd taps on my elbow and I get up from the seat, following him down the hall as Kioko waves and eases the press away a little more gently.

CHAPTER SEVEN

Lucy

You've got this. The text comes from Patty just as I'm about to throw up in the parking lot on my way in to my first day with the Pittsburgh Forge. On the one hand, this is an amazing professional opportunity, and one I almost gave up dreaming about. On the other, I made out with the team's newest player and there's just no way around that being awkward. I just have to hope he won't blab about it to the other guys.

I grab my stuff and toss the new lanyard around my neck so my ID is handy. I stare down at it again to make sure it's real. Lucy Nelson, Strength and Conditioning Coach. I'm the lone female member of the coaching and medical staff. I also happen to be the only coach who never played professionally, but as I reminded them in my interview, that's because there are far fewer opportunities for women to play soccer at that level.

Then some sort of spirit took over my body and I challenged all of them to a plyometric conditioning assessment. Todd, the head coach, laughed and offered me the job. Tawnya keeps texting me to say they were all impressed and would have hired me even if they weren't desperate to fill the role.

But I also know the team *is* desperate for help. This

morning's headlines centered around Pittsburgh's professional sports teams, as always. The baseball team is abysmal, the football team is holding steady, the hockey season hasn't started yet, and the soccer team...the soccer team has a lot going on between the move to the higher division, the doping scandal, and signing a hot-shot new star who just happens to have been born in the 'Burgh.

Maybe there won't be enough energy left to care about the new fitness coach by the time they're done picking apart Hawk Moyer.

So here I am, in my black and gold gear, crossing the threshold of my dream job, but reminding myself I'm technically here in an interim role. I'm basically auditioning for two months before they decide if they'll open up an international search. International. *Don't get too comfortable, Lucy,* I think. My phone buzzes again in my hand. I look down to see another message from Patty. ***Quit stalling and go in there like the badass I know you are. You grew a human being using just your body. Why would you let this job intimidate you?***

I grin. Patty is always reminding me that if I can raise Wyatt on my own, I can do anything. Sometimes I believe her. Other days I worry about a room full of hulking male professional athletes refusing to accept my authority, saying a bunch of sexist crap, and making my life a living hell.

Maybe that's just because my ex behaves that way.

I sigh and push open the doors, heading up to Kioko's office where I was told to report first thing. Do I feel a certain kind of way about getting a job from my teammate's husband? Yes. Yes I do, despite everyone in my life telling me to knock it off and appreciate that Kioko wouldn't have hired me if I wasn't qualified to train his team and push them into even better physical fitness.

"Is that my Lucy friend?" His booming voice carries down the hall and he meets me in a bear hug halfway between the elevator and his office. "Come in, come in and sit. I have tea for you!"

I accept the mug gratefully. I didn't get a chance for caffeine this morning between fretting about work and getting Wyatt off to daycare. Kioko grins at me. "Are you excited to get started?"

I nod, swallowing the hot liquid. He nods more enthusiastically. "Good. Good. We cannot waste a single day, you know. Now that we have been promoted we *must* play at a higher level. The players must exceed their already-great standards."

I set the cup on the desk. "I watched film and read over stats as soon as you sent over my contract. I'm ready to go observe today's practice and customize a plan for each player."

Kioko smiles. "Good. Good. I fear your predecessor did not leave us with much to go on." That's putting things politely. Apparently the guy literally pissed on his computer and shredded all his printed notes after he was fired. Kioko pats my shoulder reassuringly. "We are ready to work hard and earn our keep in the major league. Shall we go and meet the team?"

I smile. It's easy to feel relaxed with Kioko. I try to carry his reassuring energy with me as I follow him through the halls and toward the locker room. I think about my personal training clients from the gym, male and female. I've never failed to help them reach their goals, no matter how ambitious. The only reason I'm feeling any sort of jitters now is because my trash bag of an ex has messed up my head. *I am awesome at my job,* I think as I quicken my pace to keep stride with Kioko. *I can whip these men into even better shape and convince the Forge to keep me on. No matter that I was grinding my hips against the starting midfielder's crotch.*

Kioko pushes open the locker room door and pokes his head inside, motioning for me to stay back. As if I've never seen a room full of half-naked athletes. I'm about to remind him that I've seen my fair share of hairy nutsacks when I realize that Hawk might be in there, naked. I swallow and appreciate the gesture.

Kioko beckons for me to step inside with him. I hear the men shushing each other as the big boss enters the room. "Gentlemen," Kioko says with his signature smile. I've seen video of that smile he used to wear right before he blasted a kick through the goalie's outstretched fingers. "I know you'll help me welcome the newest member of our training staff. Our secret weapon, Lucy Nelson is here to make you leaner, meaner, faster, and stronger. Maybe without the mean part."

I wave. "Hi, guys. I'm ready to hit the ground running. I know you've had a rocky transition and are probably itching to up your fitness."

They nod, a few salute, and I open my mouth to finish introducing myself when I'm jostled from behind. A startled-looking Hawk mumbles an apology for nearly tripping over me and he leans back against the row of lockers, looking uneasy.

"Ah." Kioko rubs his hands together. "Now we are complete. This is our other secret weapon, Lucy. But of course you've already met Hawk Moyer."

At the sound of my name, Hawk's eyes connect with mine and there's no other way to describe his expression than "smoldering."

Kioko gestures between him and me. "Hawk and Lucy are both here to make a difference. Let's go and see what we can do, shall we?" Some of the men cheer. Coach Todd shoots finger guns and Kioko continues, saying, "Hawk, I also came to escort you back up to my office. We have business to attend to with our legal counsel. Coach, I'll have him back as soon as I can."

Coach Todd nods and blows his whistle, the shrill blast intolerable in the cramped locker room space as I watch

Hawk run a shaking hand through his hair and follow Kioko out of the room. How strange that the cocky man who gave me his number in front of my kid seems nervous to go sign some paperwork. But, then again, I did run away from him after we made out on the soccer field. Is it possible he's upset about that? I stare as Hawk walks stiffly down the hall.

Coach Todd starts yelling. "All right, men. Meet me on the field in five. Coach Lucy will be cooking up your individual torture plans later but I'm sure she's got some good full-team appetizers up her sleeve. Right, coach?" The team files out toward the field and Todd pauses by my side. He shrugs, looking at Hawk walk away with Kioko. "The good ones are always a little bit moody at the start of the season. I highly recommend you go hard on him."

He winks and I follow him out to the field, my head spinning at the effect Hawk Moyer has had on me.

CHAPTER EIGHT

Hawk

Fuck me, I'm screwed.

All week I've been fucking up on offense at practice, missing passes that I should have easily trapped...sending balls flying at inappropriate angles. I look like a damned amateur out there half the time. Now I show up in the locker room and the woman I can't get out of my head is apparently joining our coaching staff?

Coach is beaming, talking to Lucy, introducing her around. She keeps darting glances away from me, running her hands through her ponytail and acting like she wasn't pressed against me in the dark a week ago. Coach sees me squirming and I watch as he sends Lucy on out to the field with the guys.

As if that weren't bad enough, now I have to go meet a lawyer. Another man who could potentially be my father. I'm like a kid searching for the Tooth Fairy, but in reverse. Every man in his 60s could be my dad, and I feel myself recoil away from each of them ever since I set foot in this city.

I hold my breath until Kioko opens the door to his office. The lawyer guy is waiting, and he doesn't look too much older than me. I instantly relax.

"Hawk Moyer, I presume," he says, hopping to his feet,

one hand smoothing out his tie as he straightens out of Kioko's couch. He extends a hand. "Tim Stag. Pleasure to meet you." He's tall and slim with dark hair and grey eyes. I take a minute to size him up, noticing the wedding band glinting on his left hand.

I've always been comforted by the sight of wedding bands. It doesn't take a psychologist to tell me that's related to my abandonment and commitment issues. I shake Tim's hand, appreciating the firm grip we offer one another. Kioko thumps him on the back and sits on the couch next to him. "How are your little ones, Tim?"

Stag grins. "Triple trouble, just like their dad and uncles before them. Are yours doing Phenom soccer this fall?" I sit awkwardly on a chair listening to the two of them gush about their sons. Whoever this guy is, I'm guessing he's not related to anyone who'd be having unprotected sex with a teenaged drug addict. He's wearing cufflinks, for fuck's sake.

Tim turns to me and smiles. "Sorry about all that chatter, Hawk. I'll just have to see Kioko more often to catch up."

"On the sidelines of the Phenom pitch, right? Isn't your youngest about four, too?"

Tim nods, rifling through a folder in his briefcase. "Okay, Hawk, I sent these forms to your agent to look over last night. Everything is standard here. No individualized endorsement add-ons here, just your agreement with the team sponsors."

"Yeah, Brian says it all looks good?"

"All standard fare. You're committing to using Pittsburgh University healthcare and will appear in a few of their print ads for now, and we will pretend you drive a Toyota." He reaches into his shirt pocket and extracts a very fancy pen, which he uses to sign the papers before passing them to Kioko, who then passes it all to me. I like the weight of the pen in my hand. It feels symbolic somehow. Like this team and this city is heavy, but somehow fine? I don't know. I sign my name at the bottom and blow out a breath, sitting back in the chair.

"Is that it?"

Tim smiles. "Should be. From my perspective anyway. If all goes well I won't even see you again until you're up for renewal."

Kioko stands and claps another hand on my back. "All will go well. We have had enough scandal for the Forge." He squeezes my arm and I try to decide if he's making any sort of reference to me and Lucy making out. Now that she works here I guess she's even less likely to actually call me. I hate how irritated I feel about that. I remember that I'm supposed to be out on the field with the team and I make my way to my feet.

"Well, it was nice meeting you I guess." I shrug.

Tim grins. "It's fine. Kioko has my info if you run into any issues with hookers and blow."

I know he's joking, but I don't like thinking about drugs and sex workers when I'm busy brooding on my mom and my own conception. I must glower at him by accident because he holds his hands up. "My apologies. In my line of work I've had to bail *a lot* of athletes out of legal issues for…unsavory behavior."

"No worries."

Kioko waves me out of the room and I make my way down the stairs and out the tunnel to the field, where I can hear Coach blowing his whistle. I walk into the sunshine to see Lucy's ass as she leans on the fence, watching the team run sprints, with a look of extreme concentration on her face.

I have to consciously look away from her round, tempting behind as I shed my hoodie and join in with the other guys, trying not to think unprofessional thoughts about my new coach.

"Moyer!" Coach Todd frowns at me after practice. "Meet me in my office."

I nod, wordlessly, and follow him in, shutting the door behind me. It's never a good thing to get an unexpected invitation into the coach's office. I sink into the chair at his desk. He leans back into his chair, his arms crossed over his chest, pressing into the lanyard of his whistle.

We stare at each other for a few beats before he says, "What's going on in that head of yours, son?"

I blink. What am I supposed to tell him? That my game has sucked because I've been staying up all night searching the internet for evidence of the man who sired me? I have nothing to go on, not really. I just sort of…look at old newspaper articles about homeless guys to see if anyone looks like me.

Coach leans forward and folds his hands on his desk. "Moyer, I know you're new here. We're not expecting you to automatically gel with the guys. That takes time. But this past week…that's your head, and you got to tell me what's going on in there."

"Look, Coach, I know I haven't been playing my best. I'll up my time in the weight room. Direct my focus."

"Mmph." Coach makes a noise like a moose or something. "Moyer, listen to me. I'm a fixer. All you guys out there, you're delicate despite your fantastic physique. Whatever it is, I promise I've heard it before and I can help." He stares at me. I look at the ceiling. "Moyer, I've arranged for custody and visitation for guys from a bathroom stall in Louisville. I've made calls to get tattoos removed right here in the locker room before someone's wife caught sight of a mistake. Spit it out."

I pull on my hair and groan. "Shiiiiiit this is so fucking predictable."

Coach nods. "It's okay. It's affecting your game so it warrants discussion. Hit me."

I close my eyes. "I never met my father. I don't even know his name. But he's here in Pittsburgh and I can't fucking concentrate because I keep expecting to run into him in the hall or something. Like, what if he's the guy mowing the grass out there?"

My mom keeps trying to encourage me to be less angry at my father as a concept. When she met him they were both addicted to substances. Neither of them was in any sort of position to take care of a child. She couldn't even find him when she found out she was pregnant and took that as a sign from the universe that she was meant to get her act together.

I can't get past the fact that he got a free pass to carry on doing…whatever he was doing, while she was saddled with a kid and living in bum-fuck-nowhere Ohio.

"Okay." Coach claps his hands. "Deadbeat, absent father. I can work with this, Hawk. I can work with this. You ever do therapy about it?"

"What? No."

"Don't act like that. Mental health is hugely important for athletic performance." Coach points an index finger in the air. "And of course your overall well-being. But we can get you set up with someone. At minimum, you know, get Coach Lucy to write you a workout plan incorporating the punching bag." He shrugs.

I have it on the tip of my tongue to tell him Coach Lucy is the other half of my problem, that the woman I thought I'd get to take home to clear my head actually just invaded my thoughts and is now sort of my boss.

But I realize that Coach knowing that could be a pretty bad thing for Lucy, employment-wise. So instead I say, "What's her deal anyway? Coach Lucy?"

Coach grins. "She's got a stellar resume, kid. And most important, she was available on short notice." He flips open a binder on his desk. "Kioko hired her for the rest of the season as a trial run. Things work out, and she gets to keep the job and we get to not invest all our damn energy into a search for a replacement."

He leans forward conspiratorially. "Between you and me,

I'm more than ready for the press to stop hounding me about you guys and your conditioning regimen. They act like we've been Rocky IV up in here, and not the barn stuff." He shakes his head. "Lucy already started plans for each of you, customized, all that. She's sharp."

I nod. Of course she'd be sharp and focused. Is his message that I am not? "Coach, I'll get my head together. Tomorrow's training will be better."

"I look forward to that, Moyer. What are you going to do about the father situation? Your mom give you a name or anything to go from? Aw, crap, I should have asked. Your mom still in the picture?" He leans forward in the chair like he's ready to spring over the desk.

"Mom's great," I tell him, watching as he relaxes.

"Good, great. Get a name for me and I'll find the guy. Two hours and I can get you a father in here, Moyer." He holds up two thick fingers. Coach used to play defense back in his day. He's a large, intimidating man. I find myself trying to calculate his age, and then I realize there's no way he's my father. He doesn't have a gap in his resume for alcoholism and vagrancy.

"She won't speak his name," I mutter and sigh. "It always bothered me, but never so much as when I'm *here,* you know?"

He nods. "My advice? Call your mom. Get a name. Look this guy up and have it over with. Pull off the bandage, Moyer. There's a lot of games left this season. That's a lot of time with you scanning the crowd instead of reading your teammates. You hear?"

"Yes, sir."

Back at my apartment, I stare into the empty living room. So far, I've got a starter kitchen set for the food I don't cook, two stools at my counter that I think came with the apartment, and my bed. The rest of my shit is heaped around in boxes. I haven't had a chance to order anything or go shopping yet, and it's not going to happen this evening.

I pull out a box of the meals I get delivered—one of the guys on the team gave me a name of a chef that prepares everything. I just have to heat it up. While I wait for the microwave, I call my mother again.

"Hawk! I'm so excited to see you this weekend, sweetheart."

I smile, despite myself. "I'm excited to see you, too, Ma. Though I wish you'd let me get you someone to drive you here."

"Pish. I can drive a few hours on the highway. Remember, I'm going to listen to a steamy audiobook."

"Please don't, Ma." She laughs. I sigh. "Hey, so, Coach called me into his office today."

"Uh oh. Did something happen?"

I shake my head but remember she can't see me. "Not really. I've just…I'm not playing my best here."

"Well, you haven't even played a game yet, sweetheart. I'm sure you're just finding your feet."

"It's not that. It's…Ma…it's killing me knowing my father is here somewhere, roaming around." She makes a sound halfway between a sob and a groan. "I know you don't like talking about it, Ma, but I have to know who he is."

"Who he is, is my past, Hawk. I don't have to remind you how hard I've worked to change from the person I was before I had you."

"You work harder than anyone I know, Ma. But…every man in his 60s, every one I see on the street, I wonder if it's him. It's making me insane, not knowing where I come from."

"Oh, baby, I had no idea."

"Well I'm telling you now. Ma, I know he's part of your past, but he's half of my history. Hell, I can't even answer half the doctor's questions when I get a physical. Am I at risk for heart disease? Cancer? I have no fucking clue."

I hear her start to cry and I feel bad, but I'm not telling her anything I haven't said to her a thousand times before. "Let me think about it, Hawk, okay?"

"I…it's not okay. But you think about it." I hang up with her before she can get another word in.

CHAPTER NINE
Hawk

My legs are burning. I collapse onto the turf, exhausted, and I sincerely doubt I have the strength left to stand. Except I have to, because everyone around me springs back up at the sound of Coach Lucy's whistle. Turns out Lucy is indeed tough. My instincts were right about that.

I guess we need that. I just didn't expect to be in this much pain during training. It's not like I'm right out of the minors or something. I thought I was in pretty good shape. I can see Coach Todd leaning in to whisper something to Lucy as she talks to him around the whistle between her teeth. She's got us running shuttles between the goal lines, over and over. After she had us doing squats in the weight room, I might add.

I should feel relieved. The more I focus on my muscles, the less I'm searching the maintenance crew for my father or trying to convince myself to forget about Lucy Nelson.

Two of the other midfielders, Josh and Reggie, take pity on me and offer me a hand to get to my feet. "This is fucking brutal," Reggie grunts, limping a bit as we jog back to the start line.

"I'm glad it's not just me," I mutter, still trying to catch my breath.

They both shake their heads. "Naw, man, they're trying to kill us. Or Coach is trying to impress somebody."

"Or both," Josh adds, digging his toe into the turf and lining up for another round of the shuttle run.

I groan and do the same, but then I see Lucy…Coach Lucy check her watch. She blows her whistle long and loud and says, "That's a wrap, men."

Everyone cheers and starts to head through the tunnel toward the locker room, but she stands in our path. "Not so fast! You'll flood your bodies with lactic acid if you don't stretch and cool down. On your bums, legs out in front."

She doesn't have to ask me twice to sit down. I plunk onto the grass and reach for my toes, noticing the team following my lead. Lucy walks around, telling us where and how to bend and stretch, counting off until we're all breathing along with her.

I'm mesmerized by it. She stops in front of me, lifting her hand as she breathes in, pressing her palms toward the grass as she breathes out, and I breathe along with her. It feels intimate, like we're all connected. I had no idea anyone could create this sort of feeling while we're all outdoors, sprawled on the grass.

Her voice is low and calm as she tells us which muscles to stretch and I feel my body relaxing, my quads un-knotting. I've never experienced this before, breathing in unison with the team while we cool down. It's kind of…magical. I don't know how to explain it. Finally, Lucy decides we've suffered enough and sends everyone off to the showers.

I linger behind. Not because I have a sadistic urge to talk to her, but because I really can't move any faster than this slug pace. I limp slowly as she finishes her conversation with the other coaches and strides my way.

"Settling in with a little light torture," I tease her, trying not to groan as I walk.

She grins. "Is the new training regimen too much for you, Moyer?"

I love this banter we have, like she's totally comfortable

around me. I want to respond with something snarky. I want to make a sexual innuendo. But then we have to descend a few stairs and my quads practically give out on me, so all that comes out of my mouth is, "Oof." She laughs and continues walking past me.

I'm not ready to be done talking to her yet, though. I lean against a wall and tease, "I'm ready for anything you can throw at me, Lucy. Try me."

She turns to look at me over her shoulder and has the grace not to say anything about how pathetic I look after one of her workouts. "Are you always this cocky?"

I nod and pause for a second. Her brows shoot up, but I keep going. I even press off the wall so I can stand in front of her at my full height. I must smell terrible, but she wouldn't be here if she wasn't used to the smell of healthy sweat. "I told you, Lucy. It's not cocky if I can back it up." Lucy makes a face. "On the field. Obviously." I wink. She smacks me with her clipboard.

"Hit the showers, Moyer. I'll see if you've still got spare energy for jokes tomorrow."

I almost have the energy to strut into the locker room.

Josh and Reggie are barely limping anymore by the time we shower and change. They motion for me to sit with them in the film room. Hopefully this is the only time I'll watch tape of the team playing without me on the field. Coach talks us through the game against Charlotte, pausing to talk about who is out of position or who made a particularly crisp pass.

Basically none of this applies to me and I find it hard to pay attention. I watch as much as I can stand and then I step out, thinking I'll go get a drink of water or something. But when I get into the hall I hear music coming from one of the offices. Like a nosy motherfucker, I stick my head in the door and see Lucy rocking out while she makes notes on a whiteboard.

She's got all the players' names written on the board and she's making bulleted lists beneath each our names, like to-do lists. I see Reggie has "acceleration" on his list and Josh has "range of motion." I decide to make my presence known before she fills in the line beneath my name.

"Hawk. Cawky attitude," I say, leaning against her door jamb with my arms crossed over my chest.

She whips her head around and nearly drops her marker. "Jesus, Hawk. You scared me." Lucy blows a lock of hair out of her eyes and reaches for the speaker on her desk, silencing the music. "What are you doing here? Shouldn't you be in film?"

I shrug. "Felt like seeing which skills our conditioning coach was having us focus on tomorrow." I gesture at the board. "You're making notes on everyone?"

She squints. "It's literally my job to analyze everyone's performance and make a plan to improve it. So yeah. I'm making notes on everyone."

I hold my hands up. "I get it. I just wondered what you have in mind for me, that's all."

She licks her lip. "Nobody's seen you play for us yet, Mr. Moyer. You remain a mystery."

I meet her gaze coolly and she averts her eyes, suddenly fidgeting nervously. I'm not sure why I'm riding her about this. She's right—it's definitely her job to think about this shit. I guess I don't like the idea of a woman I'm interested in digging into my potential weaknesses. Which, I remind myself, is why I shouldn't be interested in this woman anymore. "You never mentioned that you were in this line of work."

She raises her brows at me. "You never asked me for my resume."

"Fair enough." I chuckle. "You're honestly telling me you haven't watched film from when I was with Utah? You have no idea what I need to work on?"

She sighs. "Of course I've watched film, Hawk. I have plans for you. Don't worry."

I open my mouth to make a snappy retort, but her phone rings and her eyes flash with concern. "Excuse me, please," she says. "I have to take this."

"Sure. I have to get back anyway." But like a dick, I make no move to retreat from her office.

She doesn't answer the call, instead walking around the desk and starting to close the door on me. I guess she's really serious about this. "I'll see you tomorrow, Hawk," she says, all but shoving me from the room. As she closes the door in my face I hear her say, "This is Lucy. Is anything wrong?"

My head immediately goes to her kid, and I want to smack myself for my inability to let it go, whatever this thing is that I feel for her. There's nothing I can do about it if there is something wrong with her son. The whole thing is none of my business. I need to focus on my game and get myself starting on the field, to earn my contract. I do not need to focus on Lucy Nelson's tongue licking her lip before she analyzes my performance. I push off the wall and limp back to the media room with the team.

CHAPTER TEN

Lucy

My new lawyer, Erika, isn't supposed to call me until next week, so when I see her name come up on my phone, I know I'm not going to like what she has to say. "I'm just going to cut to the point," she says, which…thank you. Because it costs me a few hundred dollars each time she calls. I sigh. "Nick is applying for partial custody again."

I snort. "You're joking, right?" After the hot car incident, my ex was released from the county lockup with an ankle monitoring bracelet, pending a psychological evaluation and a trial for child endangerment charges. As far as I know he is still living with his parents, and I've tried to explain to said parents that as long as they are supporting their son like this, I cannot let them see Wyatt, either. It's not possible to both endorse Nick's behaviors and support Wyatt.

Erika sighs. "I wish I were. I'm not sure what their end game is here, but the motion filed by the family claims you are alienating Nick and also leaving Wyatt unattended for your social activities."

My blood stops moving in my veins. "Leaving Wyatt unattended?" This can only possibly refer to Wyatt watching from the sidelines while I play soccer, and the only possible way he can know that is if he is following us and spying at the field.

Nick has followed me places before, mostly at work before he got barred from the property. The idea of him coming to soccer fills me with a throbbing rage. "Erika, setting aside for a minute the fact that my son is playing with other kids in a park about fifty feet away from me during soccer…what are our legal next steps here if Nick is following me? How would he know about any of this otherwise?"

Erika makes a pained sound. "Have you noticed any activity in the park that might indicate your ex is in the vicinity for work?" As an electrician, Nick would be allowed to go to job sites. But Wyatt and I have protection from abuse orders against him for putting our son's life in danger. He's not supposed to be anywhere near us.

I take some deep breaths. "I'm pretty in tune with that stuff. I would have noticed."

I hear Erika's keyboard clacking in the background as she takes notes. "He could very easily have someone else spying on you. I'm sorry, Lucy, but until we know more I don't think there is anything we can do about that issue. Let's respond to this custody motion."

She asks if anyone can vouch for me that the kids are well looked after during soccer, and I happily give her Tawnya's name. "Oh, you know Tawnya? I'll have to call her." Erika sounds pleased. I actually knew they knew one another because I debriefed Tawnya about my baggage, and she asked me who my legal counsel is. "As for the alienation part, I'm just not even going to address it for now. Our response will focus on the facts, which are that Nick cannot possibly carry out the requirements for shared physical custody when he is currently forbidden from seeing him."

My thoughts flash to the day I decided to leave Nick, when I realized I was utterly and totally under his control financially and socially. He left me at the apartment every day with no car, no money, no credit card, unless I told him in advance I would be buying groceries or clothing for Wyatt.

Erika mentioning a medical emergency calls to mind the morning Wyatt sobbed in my arms. I was sure he had an ear infection but when I walked with him to the pediatrician, I didn't have money for the co-pay. I realized both of us were in danger from Nick's iron-fisted control.

Voice shaking, I ask Erika, "Why is he even pursuing this? It's nonsensical to think someone facing child endangerment charges could get custody of that child, right?"

"Men do this shit all the time, Lucy. He doesn't actually want custody of Wyatt. He wants to make your life hard." She pauses. "Have you considered the counseling information I forwarded to you? I need you to understand that this is far from over and the mental toll these cases can take is…"

"I have the list," I tell her, cutting her off. "I just haven't had time to look into it."

"That's just it, Lucy. I know you don't have time. You're working full-time and parenting full-time and I'm sure you're compartmentalizing the shit out of the stress of having to hire me to keep you and Wyatt safe. I want to make sure you are taking care of yourself. These counselors I recommended, they're flexible. See if Naomi has openings. She offers virtual appointments."

I promise her I'll look into it and we get off the phone so she can email me the response to Nick's motion. I stare at my computer monitor, where some slime ball lawyer agreed to take Nick's money to file legal papers about this. Then I stare up at the white board, where the names of about 30 professional soccer players are staring at me, waiting for me to devise a workout plan to maximize their fitness and conditioning.

I'm sure Erika is right that I can't keep suppressing my rage at the drama in my life, but I literally do not have time to think about that right now.

Hawk's next on my list of players to plan for.

Hawk.

I also don't have time to think about him, or his cocky mouth, or his innuendos. Or that I find it all thrilling. I used to love flirting. Apparently I still do. My cheeks heat when I remember how I felt when he was teasing me, making sexy jokes. I should nip all that in the bud, but he thinks I'm interesting enough to tease, and it's been so damn long since I let myself be liked by a man. Add in a man with his perfect physique and phenomenal skill in the sport I love most in the world? I am tanning without sunscreen here.

Coach Todd asked me to go hard on Hawk. I guess he wants to try to break his spirit or something to help him fit in with the team. I can't get involved in sports psychology. That's not what I'm here for, not really. I'm also not here to moon over the star transfer like a jersey chasing fangirl.

I look down at my notes about Hawk. I've been struggling to identify a focus area for him. He has good acceleration, changes directions flawlessly, and has excellent stamina. Todd says on film, he's great with footwork and all the technical aspects of soccer. He's had a rocky first week with the Forge, but based on what I've seen, this is a hiccup. I mean, the man is here on a 7-figure contract in a sport where American players don't typically get that kind of money.

I pull up a file on my computer, a video of his last game with Utah. Hawk looks distracted on the field before the kickoff, staring into the stands. But the second the ref blows the whistle, he's all business. I relate to that mindset. I should tell Erika that soccer is my therapy right now. Like Hawk, I'm able to build tunnel vision on the field, focus on the job at hand.

I have to believe that's at least helping to stave off a mental breakdown for a little while…gah. I'm not supposed to be thinking about me right now. I have to get these plans done before it's time for me to go grab Wyatt. I take one last look at Hawk on the computer monitor as he paces backward, getting set to take a penalty kick. He's left-footed like me, brutal to defend. I like this about him, too, his relentless precision in soccer and, apparently, in his flirting. He's sort of infuriating.

That's a lie, I think as I watch him aim his hips, plant his foot, and strike the ball, which flies into the corner of the net. The camera pans to Hawk, who doesn't even seem out of breath. He's like poetry in motion, and he likes me. It's exhilarating. God, it's totally wrong for me to savor his attention, especially given the complication of me being one of his coaches. Eventually, I write "TBD" on his training plan and decide I'll come up with something he can do to loosen up his hips a bit more.

I move through the rest of the list of players with ease and finish up for the day, excited to come in tomorrow morning and put this work into action.

CHAPTER ELEVEN
Hawk

My agent wakes me with a text on Thursday. At six in the morning. I fumble around with the phone and try to call him. "You're a shit human," I say when he answers.

"You're in my same time zone now, Moyer! I can call when the news is hot."

"Does this hot news involve women or more money?"

He laughs. "No. Just giving you the heads up that you're doing a media interview today. It'll be your debut game with the Forge and the team apparently has an interim conditioning coach to replace the drug guy."

"Lucy," I mutter, scraping a hand down my face as if I can erase the dream I just had about her. It was not what you might call a professional sort of work dream.

"Come again?"

"The coach. Lucy."

"A chick? Ha!" He laughs again. "No wonder they are pulling out all the stops for media day today. It should all be pretty standard. I think the team legal counsel will be there just in case a question goes off book. Is there really a woman on the coaching staff now?"

"Is that really a big deal?"

Brian pauses. "You've played professional sports for more than a week, right? You know there isn't exactly gender

66

parity in this industry?"

"I never really thought about it." Which of course gets me thinking about it. I guess I knew I've never had any female coaches before this, but there have definitely been women in the training room in a medical capacity. Hm.

"Well. My guess is most of the questions will be going her way today, Hawkeye. Anyway, try to shave and make sure you wash your face, et cetera."

"What if I want the scruffy look to be my thing?"

"Hmmm." His pauses are getting noisier and noisier. Or am I just waking up fully? "I'll allow it. In a few weeks we're going to start wooing some watch companies for you for endorsements. Maybe some sunglasses. That shit always goes over well for dark-haired studs like yourself."

"Brian, I'm not awake enough for this conversation."

"Back to bed, then, beautiful. But still wash your face!"

I hang up on him and groan as I heft myself out of my bed. No sense falling back asleep now.

A few hours later, caffeinated and cleaned up a bit, I head up to Kioko's office to ask him if I'm supposed to be in my practice uniform or in street clothes for the media interview. The door's open and I'm surprised to see Lucy in his office, looking distraught.

"I just never had any idea I'd be speaking to the media in any capacity," she tells him. She wrings her hands as she paces around the office. "Is there any way to leave my last name out of the story?"

Kioko leans against his desk and stroke his chin. "I am sorry, Lucy, but the media is part of the package with professional sports management. Surely you knew that from your experience with collegiate teams?"

She nods rapidly and stops in the middle of the room, noticing me in the door. Her eyes glisten with tears that she really looks like she doesn't want to let fall.

"Sorry," I say. "I can come back. I just—uniform or street clothes for the presser?"

"Uniform," Kioko mutters, waving a hand. "Lucy, I'm going to call Tim Stag, our legal counsel. I'll have him speak to you and we will see what is possible. How does that sound?"

She nods and looks at me again, where I'm lingering in the door. I hold my hands up and back away, knowing when I've overstepped a boundary. Why is she so upset about the press conference? My thoughts flash back to her office the other day, where she took the worried phone call. Something isn't right with Lucy Nelson, and I know it's none of my business and I know it's not professional, but I need to find out what it is.

At first I was so focused on Lucy playing hard to get that I didn't stop to think about why she might want the getting to be hard. I'm an idiot sometimes. Lucy isn't like a jersey chaser hanging around waiting to find the Forge at night clubs. She's got a kid and, apparently, problems.

I'm surprised to realize that's not a turn off. I decide my new goal is to help her solve whatever this problem is.

CHAPTER TWELVE

Lucy

Tim Stag arrives at the stadium a few minutes after Kioko calls. He's a tall, stern-looking man in an exquisite suit, but he smiles as he shakes my hand and I feel more comfortable seeing Kioko greet him warmly.

"Lucy Nelson, this is Tim Stag of Stag Law. He handles all these sorts of things for us. Plus, he has a four-year-old son, and so do you." Kioko grins. "Doesn't that tell you all there is to know about this man?"

Tim laughs. "Great to meet you, Lucy." We all sit on the couch and I try to let my spine relax. Tim furrows his brow. "Kioko says you have some concerns about the press conference today?"

I take a deep breath. I'm not sure how much Tawnya has told Kioko and I have to weigh what I want to reveal to my new, temporary employer for whom I desperately want to work permanently. "I'm having...custody problems with my son's father," I say, biting my lip and wondering what pieces Tim can put together.

"Hm," he says, scratching at his chin. "Can you elaborate?"

I sigh. "My ex is on house arrest awaiting trial for criminally endangering our son, but his parents are wealthy and they comb through my life trying to find ways to whittle away my support, legal rights, custody, all of it."

Tim nods as I talk, cringing. "I'm so sorry you're experiencing that, Lucy," he says. He shakes his head and sighs. "Unfortunately, I'm pretty familiar with how ugly these sorts of things can get. I represent a lot of professional athletes…and there are more than a few who could work on their parenting, that's for sure."

I briefly wonder if I'll have to explain how they tried to make calls so that I wouldn't get approved for car insurance, how my lawyer had to send a cease and desist letter to Nick's family when they tried to access my medical records. Erika thinks they want to demonstrate that I'm mentally unstable. I feel mentally unstable when I consider how long I stayed in a relationship with that man.

I chew on the inside of my cheek as Tim scratches at his cheek and seems to consider the situation. "So if I'm understanding you correctly, you worry that putting yourself in the spotlight will trigger this group of individuals to somehow exploit the situation, imply you're an unfit mother, or interfere with the financial support your son is legally entitled to? Is that right?"

I relax a little into the couch, nodding. "Yes," I tell him. "That's exactly it. God, it's so validating and also embarrassing to hear you put it like that."

He frowns. "I don't see a way around getting your name out there, Lucy. Your name and title are already up on the Forge website with a photo."

"I am?" My jaw drops. I never stopped to consider my information was already out there in the public record. I snort. When would I have stopped to think about it?

"I'll attend the conference with you," Tim says. "If any of the press questions veer away from your professional qualifications, I'll wave a hand, and you just say 'no comment.' How does that sound?"

I shrug. "What do you think they'll ask me?"

Kioko slides a piece of paper across the coffee table. "This is the press release our marketing team sent ahead of time." I scan over it, looking at the bulleted list of my degree, previous experience. He says, "They might ask about the gap in employment."

We both look over to Tim for input. I don't want to bring Wyatt into this conversation at all, but I have no other explanation for that time in my life. Tim points at Kioko. "If they do that, just deflect. Interrupt, ask if anyone has more questions for Hawk. Where's the marketing director for the Forge? Are they aware of the situation?"

Tim and Kioko call in some of the other PR and marketing staff and I sit burning with humiliation while they make a game plan to help keep the media spotlight off my baggage. I feel sure that I can kiss my chances at a permanent position here goodbye. I'm causing so much extra work for all of them, just for a press conference.

Eventually we make our way into the media room, where they've set up chairs in the front for Kioko, Coach Todd, Hawk and me. Tim and the marketing guy stand off to the side and Hawk saunters in looking all moody and stubbly. He tips his chin at me and sinks into the center seat at the table. I can smell his deodorant from my seat next to him and I know it's weird, but that calms me down a bit.

It's such a normal thing. Athletes, before practice, smell like deodorant and clean laundry. This is just another day at work. I can do this. Hawk looks over at me, and he seems like he wants to ask me something, but holds back.

"What?" I say, watching out of the side of my eye as the members of the media make their way into the room. He shrugs. I frown at him. "No sexual? Not going to ask me for my number?" Then I gasp, holding my hand over the microphone. I realize it's not on yet and I chastise myself for being so careless, especially after I was the cause of urgent last-minute planning meetings for this conference I'm sure they thought would be par for the course.

"I always want your number, Lucy," he whispers. And then he winks at me. I swear, I feel it in every pore of my body. I can't decide if he means it or if he knew how much I needed the distraction. Before I have time to decide, Kioko claps his hands and welcomes the press to the stadium. Todd, Kioko, and the press corps could have heard any of this. I clench my fists and try to regain composure. I cannot talk like this with Hawk. Not here.

The questions start firing in. Is the team ready to face Baltimore this weekend? Has Hawk been able to learn all the plays in his short time here? Does the Forge feel Hawk was worth the significant financial investment they placed in his contract? "Yes," Kioko says with a smile. "Absolutely."

I start to relax, especially as the questions center around Hawk and his adjustment to Pittsburgh. He even shares that he became friendly with some of his neighbors, and they are giving him the inside scoop on good coffee and excellent auto mechanics. He's charming in a way that seems to contrast the gruff exterior he's shown on the field and interacting with the staff here.

Finally, the questions pivot to the team's strength and conditioning and I'm called on to verify details about my background, what it's like being a woman on the all-male staff. "Can you clarify the question," I ask, taken aback.

The reporter frowns. "You know, everyone else is male…what's that been like for you?"

I think of the Phe-Moms, how we often have to kick men off our field when we have the permit and they want to just show up and play soccer. Men seem to feel so entitled to spaces and fields and jobs… I try to imagine how Patty would answer this question and I say, "Well, they all seem to follow my advice so far. I have, after all, worked with male athletes in teams and individually."

"Yes, about your former team coaching experience." The *Post* reporter flips through his notepad and smirks. "Lucy, what made you resign from your position with Pittsburgh University? Does the Forge have any cause to worry you'll step down mid-season?"

I furrow my brow, seeing Tim waving frantically from the sides as Kioko shifts in his seat. "I just got here," I say into the mic. "I have no plans to go anywhere." Feeling emboldened, I continue. "As you know, I'm in an interim role, but I hope the players' improved performance will demonstrate the value of signing me on full-time."

Kioko smiles at me and gives me a thumbs up below the table. I start to relax a little more. I almost slouch in my seat. The same reporter turns to Hawk. "Speaking of longevity in Pittsburgh...Hawk, you confirmed that you were actually born here in Pittsburgh and we were able to verify public birth records. Then we did a little more digging...care to comment on your relationship with your father, who still lives in the area?"

Hawk turns white. "We are not in contact." He glares at the reporter, who stares at his notes, still smirking.

"That's interesting, considering your brother seems to be handling your legal contracts and managing the negotiation to get you here on the Forge. No inside baseball with your biological family?"

I watch as the bones seem to fall out of Hawk's body along with the color in his skin. "Excuse me?"

"Ted Stag," the reporter says, checking his notepad. "Your father. Do you care to comment on your relationship with him? I notice you don't share a last name."

CHAPTER THIRTEEN
Hawk

"The fuck did you just say?" The question comes from Tim Stag, standing to the side of the room, near Lucy. He looks like he wants to dive into the audience and strangle the reporter asking the questions.

The guy grins and raises a brow at Tim. I try to remember how to breathe. Did he just say my father's name? The reporter says, "Ted Stag is the biological father of Hawk Moyer. We confirmed this from several sources at a rehabilitation clinic and a social services organization who worked with homeless populations. The readers of the *Pittsburgh Post* want to know if they're still in touch and how the Stag family feels about the return of their long-lost brother."

I don't even have to say anything. Tim storms over to the wall and yanks on the cord to the power strip for all the mics. "This press conference is over," he yells, his face turning red and his nostrils flaring.

I cross my arms over my chest, trying to figure out which emotions I'm feeling, or if it's possible to just have all of them at once. The shock is so intense I feel like I'm going to fly out of my body. Ted Stag is my father's name? Stag like Tim Stag? Kioko clears the room and I jump when I feel a hand on my arm. It's Lucy's. I stare down at her fingers on my bicep.

"Are you okay? What's going on?"

I shake my head and glance over her shoulder to where Tim is screaming, but trying not to scream, at the PR and marketing staff. He evidently feels the reporter should have given the team a heads up if they were going to pursue that line of questioning. I swallow and turn my attention back to Lucy, wondering why her hand is still on my arm and if I could possibly convince her to keep it there. "So my birth father lives here in Pittsburgh," I tell her. "He's a piece of shit."

She nods. "I know a little bit about that sort of thing," she says. Her touch is grounding me and I'm able to think.

"I never even met him. My mother never told him about me. That's how little my mother wanted him involved in my life." Lucy starts rubbing my arm now and it makes me want to tell her everything, anything, just so she'll continue touching me like this, soothing me. She just navigated her own stressful crap and she's somehow finding the ability to offer me comfort right now. I need it.

She frowns. "Does the press ask the other players about their families?" She looks over her shoulder where Tim has his phone in hand and is yelling things about slander and libel.

Her questions keep me grounded, which is good because I feel like I'm going to sink through the floor. I shrug, trying to figure out why this reporter was so invasive at a standard presser. "I think any time a pro athlete is playing for their hometown team, they do. Not that I consider Pittsburgh my hometown."

"Hawk!" Kioko shouts from the doorway. "Upstairs with me, if you please. Coach Lucy, you may go proceed with practice." He pauses to smile at her. "When you are ready."

Lucy pats my arm and waves. "See you out there, okay? I'll make sure you get caught up on the extra sprints."

I groan and rise to follow Kioko, who is now in the hallway waiting for the elevator with Tim Stag, who looks like he swallowed something electric. *Ted Stag,* the reporter said. Holy shit. It's all starting to sink in now, but the edges of the picture are still fuzzy as my brain tries to work it all out. Do I seriously have a name for the absent figure in my life? Tim is tugging on his hair and muttering something about "should have known" and "should have fucking assumed." He finally seems to realize I am in the room and whips his head around to me. "Did you know?" He points a finger at me and steps closer. I edge back.

"Did I know what? That my deadbeat father lives in Pittsburgh? Yeah. I also know I've never met him and he left my pregnant mother to die under a bridge. What of it?"

His eyes narrow and a vein in his neck looks like it's going to burst as it pulses. "Ted Stag," he hisses, "is my father, too."

Kioko finally manages to get me and Tim into the elevator and into his office, where I collapse onto the couch and Tim commences pacing the room. Tim Stag. My brother.

I stare at him, trying to decide if we look alike, if I should have noticed. Should I have felt some sort of connection to him? Like, should I have known in my cells?

I have a brother. Not only do I have a father out here somewhere, but I have a sibling. "Are there more of you?"

I direct the question at Tim and realize it doesn't make any sense because he's not inside my head working through this chain of events. But he must catch my drift because he pauses and frowns. "I have two brothers, yes. Do you not read the news? Truly?"

"The news?" I snort. "All I usually read is my training plan. Why should I know about your brothers, exactly?"

Tim scoffs and resumes pacing, muttering to himself. Kioko approaches him and suggests he call his wife, which halts Tim in his tracks. "Yes. Alice. Of course. I should call Alice." I watch as he sinks into the couch and calls his wife, how he seems to calm down immediately upon hearing her voice. It's surreal, listening to him tell her, "My father must have had an affair after he left us…Yes, Ted. We have a fucking brother, Alice. A secret Stag."

Kioko places a hand on Tim's back and he swats him away, then lowers the phone and looks at me. "Will you agree to a DNA test?"

"What?"

"A DNA test. To verify the reporter's allegations."

I look up at Kioko. "Look, man, I'm having a little bit of a stroke right now. Nobody is sticking a swab in my nose until I understand what just happened."

Kioko repeats that a reporter apparently interrogated anyone he could find in connection with my mother, that a few people told him the name of the guy she'd been sleeping with when she was a teenager.

"A teenager! Christ! Fuck!" Tim screams and roars as he paces around the room and then stops abruptly with the phone against his ear, and nods his head. "You're right, baby. No, I don't need you to come by. You're right. Yes," he says. "Yes, maybe it would be good to send someone else. Can you ask Donna to do that for me?"

He hangs up with his wife and kicks a trash can, reminding me of my own proclivity toward angry outbursts. At least I can go kick some balls around when I'm this pissed. Not that I am able to move from this couch right now.

Tim drags his palms down his cheeks and makes his way over to me, squatting down. "I owe you an apology. My father is a sore subject of conversation for me and, as you can imagine, this news upset me a great deal."

I nod at him, just the tiniest movement of my head. "Half my existence is a black hole," I growl at him. "Just darkness. Nothingness. No name, no nothing." We stare at each other a few minutes. "And I could have had brothers." My voice is a whisper. Tim nods and swallows.

He looks up at Kioko. "Kioko, my friend, please excuse me. I was unforgivably rude." Kioko waves a hand, leaning against the window. Tim gathers up some of his things. "I'm bringing in another member of Stag law. I'm no longer able to be partial in assessing contracts related to the Forge or to Mr. Moy—to my brother."

"That seems like a nice solution for paperwork," Kioko says. "But Tim, I am concerned for you as my friend. This is a very big shock. And Hawk, I was not aware this could be a problem. Are you okay?"

"Well, no, I'm not okay, sir. I need a few minutes, to be frank."

Kioko nods and mumbles something about more scandal, more bad press for the team. I start to wish I could sink into the   sofa   and   disappear.

CHAPTER FOURTEEN

Lucy

As I walk away from the press conference, my heart aches a bit for Hawk, and for my own son. I see the hurt in Hawk's eyes and know there is nothing anyone can do to repair or replace the love he should have had from his father. No wonder he's been moody, if he moved to a city where he knows his father is living, unaware he even has another son.

In twenty years, will Wyatt have this sort of chip on his shoulder? If Nick produces more children, will Wyatt mourn the loss of knowing them? I know it doesn't make sense, but I feel like, somehow, if I can be there for Hawk as he navigates this pain, I'll feel more in control. I pause in my office, gathering my notes and my whistle, and decide there's nothing I can do about Wyatt's future anger at his father. I'm angry at Nick, too. I think back to Erika's insistence that I speak to someone professionally, so that my anger doesn't simmer and pressurize. I think today's press conference gave me a preview of what might happen if I don't prioritize her advice.

I look at the sheet of counselors Erika gave me, but it all seems like too much, all those names. The idea of calling them all, waiting for calls back, disrupting my day again and again just to get set up. I shake my head. I'm not ready for that right now. I have work to do here, to secure my place so I have hope of someday soon having the capacity to deal with my own shit.

I walk out to the field, where Todd has the men warming up by running laps. I groan. I had a whole plan in place to warm up with hip openers and plyometric exercises to loosen the players' knee joints. I blow my whistle. "All right, Forge, stop where you are and walk to me, please."

Todd's eyes widen in confusion as he looks at me, but I tap my clipboard, which he has a copy of because I set it on his desk before I left yesterday. I call the team back in and lead them through the exercises I had planned, gently stretching them while they're in motion, reducing the risk of them injuring their muscles and tendons. Once I feel like they're sufficiently limber, I pat Todd on the shoulder. "They're all yours," I say.

He just stares at me again, but then eventually nods and splits them into groups based on their positions. I take my usual stance by the fence, observing. And then I smile because as I watch, Reggie's acceleration seems to have improved. *I can do this,* I think. When I assert myself here confidently, like when I took back over the training session, I'm making good things happen. I'm getting results.

For years, since I found out I was pregnant, I've felt like a person things happen *to.* I don't want to be like that anymore. I want to be a person who makes things happen.

Starting with this job. I want to make them beg me to stay here.

A few minutes later, I see Hawk emerge from the locker room, his jaw clenched. I realize how touched I am that he confided in me in the swirl of that press conference. My instinct is to go over and put an arm around him, tell him to take the day off and process what just happened to him. But the fact that he's out here seems to mean he wants a sense of normalcy right now. Or maybe to process his feelings through motion. He runs over to where Todd has the guys divided into teams to scrimmage and I observe as he's placed in the left midfield position.

I try to watch all of the players, making notes on my chart to assess their progress in different metrics. I'd be lying if I said I wasn't more focused on Hawk, though. I wish I could go touch his arm again, check in with him. He's playing furiously, sprinting all out to every ball, whipping every pass just a little too hard so it ricochets off the recipient's foot or thigh.

Each time he makes an error, Hawk seems unable to let it slide off him, instead growling and clenching his fists. I'm sure all the guys have heard about the press conference by now, whether from Coach Todd or from Jacques, the captain. Nobody says a word to Hawk about his playing. After about an hour, Todd turns things over to me to move the men through weight training.

We reconvene in the weight room and I pass out the worksheets for their individual training plans. "We're just going to do baseline testing today," I explain. "We need to find out what your max weight is on each of the main Olympic lifts so I can figure out what percentage of that weight you should be using for each exercise."

The men look at me like I'm speaking a foreign language. Which, I suppose for a lot of them who've come here from other countries, I am. I sigh and point to Reggie. "Okay, so, Reggie is going to deadlift until he can't lift any more weight. What do you usually lift, Reg?"

He grins and tells me 200 pounds. I sigh and stick a 45-pound plate on each side of the bar. "Let's start here and work up." They all watch me as I set up different stations to work them through dead lifts, squats and power cleans. It takes ages to correct their form. The absence of a strength and conditioning coach seems to have them all phoning it in with these exercises. All of them apart from Hawk, who has taken a seat on the rowing machine and begun to churn out a blistering pace.

I let him work through his feelings while I get the rest of the team situated and then I reach for the handle, stopping him. "You're not going to get an accurate baseline test if your muscles are fatigued like this." I raise a brow at him.

He shrugs. "I missed warmups. It's fair compared to what they already did."

I laugh. "You think I worked them this hard before the scrimmage?" I glance at the dash on the rowing machine. "You're working through a lot of big feelings there, champ."

"You mispronounced my name, Lucy." His eyes flash at me with something…not anger. Is he about to flirt with me? He nods toward my clipboard. "You ever going to tell me what's on my to-do list for improvement?"

I squat down so I'm level with him and I put a hand on his. "Look, Hawk, what happened at the press conference was upsetting. Do you have someone to talk with?"

He frowns. "You were pretty upset there yourself, Lucy. Want to tell me why you're so afraid of the limelight?"

I bite my lip. "That's none of your business."

His eyes flash again, colder this time. "Yeah, well my daddy drama is none of yours. Now give me a workout or I'm going to keep making up my own."

Him shutting me out stings. We stare at each other for a few beats before I rip a piece of paper from my pad. I scribble "Row to hell." I slap the paper onto his knee and return my focus to the members of the team who are ready to listen to my   advice.

CHAPTER FIFTEEN
Hawk

Brothers. I have brothers. Three of them, from the sound of things. After practice, I drive home to sit in my still-nearly-empty apartment, staring at a wall.

My entire life I have hated my father, barely respected my mother's decision to keep his name from me. I could have done what this reporter from the *Post* did or like Coach suggested...I could have hired someone to dig. I could have done that any time. I didn't bother because I thought I was just ignoring the existence of a man who wasn't worthy of knowing my name.

But I could have had brothers.

I pick up my phone and pull up a web browser, typing Stag Pittsburgh into the search engine. Whatever I expected to find there, the results are a thousand times more surprising. My brother Tim owns Stag Law. I knew this, but didn't realize what a big deal it is. His law firm represents all the professional sports teams in the city, handles their endorsement contracts, all of it. And Tim is big into philanthropy and community service so there are hundreds of news articles about him.

No wonder that reporter looked like a bear discovering a honeycomb. I feel a twist of rage in my guts that the reporter seems out to besmirch my brother's name. I hated how he brought up my contract negotiations like that.

I scroll down to a picture of Tim with his arms around two other guys that look like him. He apparently runs marathons with his brothers Tyrion and Thatcher. Like, a lot of marathons. "Timber, Tyrion and Thatcher Stag." I practice saying their names out loud, not knowing if I'll ever have cause to do so again.

Tyrion, who goes by Ty according to the news, was a pro hockey player who retired to be a stay-at-home dad for his four sons. His wife is some kind of big-deal trial judge. Four sons. I guess that means I have…nephews. I drag my fingers through my hair. I've never had family. It's just been me and my mom my entire life. Her extended family wasn't too keen on maintaining relationships with the daughter who flunked out of college to become a junkie and a pregnant teenager.

Our community in Loudonville consisted mostly of Mom's friends from church and my soccer teammates. Brothers and nephews were things my teammates had, things I felt bitterly jealous of every holiday and every regular weekend day when everyone else had huge cheering sections in the stands for them and plans to suck down family dinner after our weekend matches.

My brother Thatcher is an artist. There's a big shift in the media coverage of him, showing his maturity from a playboy to a family man. He's got a wife and kids, too.

I throw my phone down on the sofa next to me. The three of them had each other to lean on, to talk to. And I'm some dirty secret they never had to think about. I remind myself that if it's true what my mom says about my father's alcoholism, chances are pretty good he was a shit dad to them. But they knew he was shit. They never had to wonder, never had a big black hole sucking up half of their identity.

"FUCK," I scream into the empty apartment.

And then, like it heard me, it beeps at me. *No, it's not the apartment beeping*, I think. It's the intercom. Someone's at the door. I'm sure as hell not in the mood for company, but I flick the button on the video doorbell to see who it is pushing the button. My eyes widen when I see it's no other than Tim Stag. "What are you doing here?" I don't bother with small talk.

"Just let me up," he says, treating me with the same attitude. I buzz him in, propping the door open and leaning against the frame while I wait for him to emerge from the elevator.

He steps out a minute later, still wearing his suit and tie, but looking frazzled. He twists his wedding band around his finger rapidly and his eyes dart side to side like he's looking for spies or something. "Can I come in?"

I step back from the door and close it behind him when he enters. I'm still not settled in so the apartment is still pretty sparse. We sit on the pair of stools that came with my counter and I stare at him, my brother. It's going to take me a long time to get used to thinking that.

He stares back at me. "We need to talk," he says and I spit out a laugh.

"No shit, *brother*." I emphasize the last word like I'm not sure whether it's a curse.

Tim sighs. "I don't know what you know. I'm guessing not much."

I breathe out through my nose. "All I knew was that I was born in Pittsburgh and my teenaged mom got knocked up by some drunk who she says wasn't worth telling about my existence."

Tim strokes his growing stubble while I talk and I realize I'm doing the same thing. I snap my hand down into my lap. Tim takes another deep breath. "Our mother died when I was a teenager. It was very sudden and my father…did not take it well. He abandoned us for the bottle." I glare at him. "I mean that literally," Tim continues. "I've been my brothers' only parent for a long time."

"So you don't know where he is?" I realize that I sort of hope the man died and as I'm listening to Tim talk about how hard his life was having to raise himself and two little brothers, I don't even feel bad about it.

"We know," he says. "*Now.* Thatcher found him a few years ago when he was dying."

I scoff. "That's awfully convenient. For him."

Tim grins at me. "That was my reaction at the time." He explains that Ted Stag finally got sober and has gradually been easing back into their lives. He tells me his brothers are quicker to forgive than he is. "I don't know if you have any interest in connecting with him," Tim says, and then leans forward, resting his elbows on the counter and staring into my eyes. "But I'd really like it if you could meet Ty and Thatcher. My...our...brothers."

I swallow a huge-ass lump in my throat. "I'd like that, too. But I'm not, you know, ready to meet ... Ted."

Tim grunts. "I'm not ready to see that fucker again any time soon, either. Don't tell my wife I called him that."

"I haven't met your wife, man."

Tim grins. "You should. She'd help shape your perspective on everything. It's annoying."

I nod. "Sometimes a man just wants to sit and brood about things."

Tim squeezes my leg. "We're a lot alike, Hawk."

I stare at my big brother some more, not sure what to say.

CHAPTER SIXTEEN

Lucy

I hear the reporter's voice from the news as I finish getting dinner for Wyatt. *"Drama today at the Forge stadium as a run-of-the-mill press conference ends in controversy. Star player Hawk Moyer and Stag Law CEO Tim Stag angrily ejected members of the media from the stadium as team officials decline to comment on the—"*

I mash the buttons on the remote, finally changing the channel to PBS. The theme song to *Octonauts* fills the apartment instead and I return to my thoughts as I microwave Wyatt's pasta. I acted unprofessionally. I let my temper overtake my composure at work when one of my athletes was rude and it's my responsibility to train him. "It's literally my job to put up with his shit," I mutter.

I get Wyatt settled in with a movie and step into the bathroom to call Hawk. "'lo?" His voice warbles.

"Hawk? Are you okay?"

"Lucy the milf," he drawls, his words sounding slurred. "Loooooooooosey."

"Holy shit, are you drunk? We have a game tomorrow!" I hiss at him into the phone and look at my watch. It's a bit after six. I start to calculate the time between now and when the team has to present for warmups tomorrow. "Jesus, Hawk. What's gotten into you?"

I hear him belch. "Didya know I've got brudders?"

I sigh. Right, the press conference. I open the door to peek at Wyatt and bite my lip. I've got to do something. "Don't drink any more alcohol, okay? Where are you?"

"Echo, echo, echo," he says, then giggles. "It's empty here. I don't even have a couch."

"Are you at home? Hang tight. I'm coming over."

I step into the hall and tap on my neighbor's door. The elderly tenant lives alone and I sometimes grab milk or cat food from the store for her. She's often offered to watch Wyatt for me, but I've never taken her up on it. Now feels as good a time as any to ask.

She opens the door wearing a nightgown and slippers but I hear the television blaring in the background. "Hi, Gladys," I wave. "Would I be able to ask you to hang out with Wyatt for an hour while I take care of a friend?"

Her eyes light up. "Sure," she says, smiling and putting on her robe. "You've got a sweet boy there, Lucy. I'm happy to help."

I choke back a wave of emotion at her sincerity and get her situated on my couch next to Wyatt, who spoils the plot of the movie for her.

I slip out quietly to look Hawk's address up in his file, and remind myself I have access to this file because I'm in a position of authority at his workplace. He lives close by, and I realize I could walk if I wanted. We're almost neighbors. Faster to drive, though.

When I get to Hawk's building, I'm relieved that someone is coming out the front door as I rush up to it, so I don't even have to buzz and wait for him to amble over to the intercom.

I tap on his door. "Hawk," I whisper-shout. "It's Lucy. Can you let me in?"

The door cracks open a minute later and Hawk squints at me. "You're really here?"

I roll my eyes. "Yes, you big lug. Come on, let's get some

food into you." I push the door open and he wobbles backward. "What did you drink?"

He shrugs, following me to his kitchen. "Buncha beers." He belches again.

"Okay, that's not as bad as it could be. Although you're going to be wrestling with some bloat tomorrow." I click my tongue at him.

He pats his stomach and looks down. "Still hard as a rock. Wanna feel?" He lifts his shirt and rubs his abs. I will not stare at his abs. No I will not.

"Hawk." I use my mom voice. "I am here to help you sober up and maximize your chances to play well tomorrow. Sit." I point at the stool and throw open his fridge. He's got a stack of packaged meals in there, and I sigh in relief as I grab one and shove it in the microwave. I don't see any sports drinks, so I pour him a glass of water and root around my purse for some aspirin.

"Take this." He gives me a feeble salute and starts to chug the water. Another belch. The microwave bings and I slide him a plate of food. When I open his drawer there is one single set of silverware, and I sigh at the sight, but grab him the fork. "And this."

I laugh a little when I think he tries to make a sexy face, but ends up stabbing himself in the lip with the tines of the fork. He chews a few bites and I lean my elbows on the counter, observing. "I'm sorry I was mean to you at training," I tell him. "That was unprofessional of me and I apologize."

"Row to hell," he murmurs and grins. "Like go to hell. You're funny."

I sigh and shake my head, checking my watch. I can stay a few minutes before I have to get back to Gladys and Wyatt.

Hawk catches my eye and makes a pained face. "Does Wyatt know his father?"

The question hits me like a shot to the chest. I nod rapidly and swallow. "Yes, he does."

"Will you tell me what happened?" Hawk taps his temple with his fork. "You're not with him...I can tell."

A chill washes over me at the thought of rehashing my experiences with Nick. But I remind myself Hawk is vulnerable when it comes to fathers. I swallow and reach for Hawk's water glass, taking a sip. "He never physically abused me, but I'm certain he would have started eventually." Hawk clenches his jaw, his hands curling into fists. "By the time I left he was controlling every aspect of my life. All the money. He was going out to the car each night to check the odometer. If I went somewhere, he demanded to know who I talked to and what lies they spread about him." I shiver.

"When I left, I took nothing. Just Wyatt. Our pediatrician helped us get to the women's shelter, and they connected me with grants to pay rent." I stare past Hawk as I relay the process of applying for food stamps and using the shelter's lawyer to set up our original custody and visitation orders.

I watch Hawk's throat as he swallows, his gaze serious, unflinching. He sounds more sober when he asks, "Is it better now? Now that you left?"

I feel a lurch in my stomach, knowing how intently he's listening to me even amidst his turmoil. I close my eyes and shake my head in response to Hawk's question. "His family condones his behavior. He lives with his parents now and they make it their part-time job to harass me in every way imaginable. They called my old job to claim I was acting inappropriately with male clients. They call child protective services and claim my car or home are unsafe. Nick used to show up for visitation when he felt like it and skip when he didn't, but if I was ever 30 seconds late, they called the police to try to hold me in contempt."

Hawk's eyes flash as I talk. I can tell the food and water and time have helped dampen his drunkenness. He seems to be listening to me more seriously. I run my hands through my hair and sigh. "It took me a long time to sever all ties they held over me. But every cop in Zone 4 knows me, I have a good job now, and a new lawyer helping me try for full and exclusive custody."

Hawk nods at this last bit. "Thank you for telling me all that," he says, earnestly.

"You're welcome." We stare at one another for a few beats. It feels so good to tell him some of these things. I've been carrying all this on my own for so long. To have him open up to me in return feels like everything right now, even if he is three sheets to the wind.

"I didn't ever think about how hard it was for my mom to be with an alcoholic," he says. He reaches a hand for me and then seems to reconsider, putting it on his lap. "I've always been so angry at her for keeping me away from my father."

His eyes still have a glassy quality telling me he's still got a ways to go toward sobering up. I shove his plate toward him again and he takes another bite. "I'm sure she was only thinking of what was best and safest for both of you," I tell him. "I know it in my bones." Hawk nods and closes his eyes. "Will you tell me about her?"

He turns his head toward me and I smile, because he looks rumpled and real right now, not like he's trying to be charming. More like he looked when we were running around together on the soccer field.

He says, "I used to try to quit all my soccer teams so I could pick up part-time jobs. She would always head me off at the pass and tell all my coaches she had things handled." He takes a bite of his food. More sober now, he tells me they eventually reached a compromise in the summers and he worked roofing jobs under the table.

"How old were you? Roofing?" I shudder, thinking about Wyatt climbing around up on people's high roofs.

He shrugs. "Fifteen? I brought home a lotta cash, Lucy. A lot. And roofing is a good workout."

I make an incredulous noise. "You were probably

dehydrated. Did you get sun stroke?"

He grins. "I got so tan. You wanna see my tan lines?"

"Hawk."

He drops the fork and puts his head in his hands before looking at me again. "Fuck those days, though. All those ladders, hauling shingles. Fuck every tear my mother shed, too."

I see a tear form in the corner of one of his eyes and resist the urge to reach out and wipe it away. "I have brothers," he whispers. "I could have grown up with brothers."

"Hey." I reach out and touch his chin, lifting his face to meet his dark eyes. "You can still have a relationship with your brothers. There's nothing stopping you from that."

The next time I see Hawk, he's on fire on the field, starting at midfield for the Forge for the first time. The team's marketing manager provides prepared statements for the press before the match so none of the players or coaches have to talk with the media.

I stand on the sideline with Coach Todd, nodding and taking notes as the Forge gel on the field. Something about the atmosphere of competition rather than just practice has turned a switch on inside Hawk. He streaks up and down the field, transitioning deceptively between offense and defense. He owns the left channel, appearing out of nowhere to intercept passes from Baltimore and quickly transfers the ball to Reggie or Josh. While most of the team plays with joy on their faces, dominating the game from the first whistle, Hawk wears an intense expression.

I try not to think about how sexy he looks, all sweaty and brooding as he plants his right foot in the grass, swings and shoots a ball into the goal from 20 yards out. I try to think about the mechanics of his glorious thigh muscles, his trim calves. I can't let myself lust after the man who was so vulnerable last night, who listened so intently as I poured my guts out talking about my ex.

He takes his jersey off and whips it around his head, sweat glistening in the dark curls on his chest as he cheers. I swallow thickly from the sidelines, extremely turned on and not sure what to do about it. I force myself to ignore the flutter in my belly when the final whistle blows and Hawk turns toward me on the sideline. His eyes meet mine and for a brief moment, he smiles before the team crashes around him to celebrate.

CHAPTER SEVENTEEN
Hawk

"Hey, man, that was a great pass." I slap Reggie on the back in the locker room after the match. He turns and looks at me, his expression strange.

"Thanks, Hawk."

"Yeah, man. Of course." The room is buzzing with excitement. I should feel more excited about the win but I'm still carrying around a lot of the weight of yesterday's big reveal. I take a minute to wonder if my brothers watched the game, and then I get angry for hoping they had, even if they haven't met me yet.

I can't have any expectations about any of this. It's going to fuck with my head and that's going to fuck with my career. Christ, why couldn't Brian have just sealed a deal with Columbus? None of this would have happened.

Coach sticks his head into the room, a grin on his face. "Men! Shower up. Coach Lucy says go easy on the booze tonight." He winks and heads back into the hall. Around me, I hear the guys talking about which clubs they'll hit up on the South Side, which is evidently the city's hot neighborhood for nightlife.

I yank off my cleats and hurry through a shower, not wanting to lose myself in the bass tonight at a club. I know if I go to one of those places I'll drink way too much and make bad choices. I've been doing enough of th the past few weeks.

"Hawk, you going to the club with us?" Josh t s his dark arms across his chest, already decked out in Tom d and a flashy watch.

I shake my head while pulling on a clean shirt. "So I'm still in my head a little. I can't tonight." I push open the into the hall and a tiny human crashes into me, wrapping a around my legs. I look down to see Lucy's kid hugging me.

"Hawk! That was amazing! You scored a GOAL!" He grins up at me with eyes shining and I see that he's wearing the jersey I signed for him my first night in town.

"I'll catch you later then," Josh says, giving me a salute as he and a group of the guys head out together.

I crouch down and offer Wyatt a high five. "Thanks, pal. Fans like you make it worthwhile." I peer over his shoulder, not seeing Lucy. "Where's your mom?"

"She's in her office. I'm not supposed to touch anything." I nod and stand up, offering him a hand and he wraps his pudgy fingers around mine.

"Let's get you back down there, okay?" I walk the few feet to her office, where her door is ajar and she's fluttering around the room organizing paperwork.

"Wyatt, just a few more minutes," she says over her shoulder, not looking up.

"Aw, man," I say, making a pout face at Wyatt, which makes him laugh. Lucy whips her head around.

"Hawk!" She seems to pull herself together and takes a deep breath. "Aren't you going out to break in-season diet rules with the rest of the team?"

I grin, feeling suddenly like I won the after-game celebration, too. "I'd rather take Wyatt out for ice cream." It's a dick move, using her kid to get to Lucy, offering him ice cream without asking her first. But I never said I was a nice guy.

"Ice cream? Mom, can we?"

She furrows her brow at me and her nostrils flare. "I'm sure Mr. Hawk wasn't being serious, honey. I've got some cookies at home we can have."

"I'm super serious," I tell her. And a thought occurs to me. "Hey, Wyatt, you know what? I haven't ridden on that thing that goes up the mountain behind the stadium. I see that on billboards and tourist stuff all about this city. Do you know anything about that?"

His face lights up. "The Incline! Yes! There's ice cream up there. Mom, Hawk's gonna take us on the INCLINE!"

Lucy mutters something under her breath and yanks her backpack from her desk chair. She pokes a finger into my shoulder. "You'll pay for this in sweat, Hawk."

She shakes her head and then gives a small smile before hurrying down the hall after Wyatt, who is literally skipping toward the parking lot. We step into the night and I feel the breeze from the river. It's gorgeous, clear skies and the summer heat has given way to that crisp coolness of autumn. "How are we getting there?" I forgot about car seats when I suggested this adventure.

Wyatt giggles and points to the path ahead. "We walk, silly! Past the big wheels!" There's a fleet of paddle wheeled river boats parked near the stadium and beyond that, I see a pedestrian walkway over the highway, leading up to the Incline. The iconic red cars move on rails in opposite directions up the steep angle of Mt. Washington, originally built to help transport mill workers I guess.

"Imagine having to take this home from work in a factory?" I look up overhead as one of the cars descends to get a fresh wave of passengers.

Lucy shrugs. "A lot of people still do ride it to commute. But I guess they're mostly going downtown to work in offices or hospitals these days." We make our way over the road and up the steps to the ticket booth.

I step up to the window before Lucy can fish around in her bag for her wallet and grab 3 round-trip tickets. "It was my idea, so I should pay," I tell her. Wyatt is jumping up and down, peeking through the window at the gears on the tracks, waiting for the next car.

Lucy wraps an arm around his shoulders, pulling him back when it arrives and unloads a car full of people dressed up for a night out. They noisily make their way out into the night and Lucy lets Wyatt loose inside the car. He jumps to the back, where he presses his hands and face against the glass, ready to watch as we ascend.

I take a seat next to him and Lucy watches me strangely as I put a hand on his back to steady him when the car groans into motion. I shrug. "I don't want him to fall."

"No," she whispers. We all look out the window as the car climbs the hill. This city sure does put on a show at night, lit up skyscrapers and stadiums, all of it reflecting off the water of the rivers that converge at Point Park.

"It's so pretty," Lucy says to Wyatt, stroking his cheek. "We have a beautiful city, huh?"

He nods and points to the science museum. "We're going there! On a field trip!"

She smiles at him. "That's right. Kioko is taking you to tour the submarine, huh?"

As the car reaches the top and slows it occurs to me that I'm a professional athlete at the peak of my career, declining a night out in a slick club in order to talk about submarines with a four year old and a beautiful woman. I decide that this is actually an amazing way to spend the evening until I remember that Lucy is technically my boss. And she doesn't want me that way, the way that leads to moans and gasps and slick bodies pressed together.

I sigh as Wyatt bursts out of the car, shouting for me to follow him to look at the gears through the window in the upper station. We look at the historic photographs on the walls and he shows me pictures of old floods and the city's industrial history.

"Okay," he says, putting a hand on his hip and making me laugh. "Now we go outside and take pictures on the platform."

"Is that right?" I love how he's pretending to be a tour guide. Hell, I need a tour guide. I haven't done anything like this since I moved here. It's nice getting a sense of the city where I was born. I try to tamp down the other feelings I have about those circumstances and appreciate how amazing it is to look down the mountain at the colors and lights.

"Okay, this is where you lean on the fence and take a selfie," Wyatt says, pointing. I do as he says and grin.

"I'll send this to my mom," I tell him and Wyatt's eyes get wide.

"You have a mom?"

"Ha! Sure, kid. Just like you have a mom." I wink at Lucy and she flushes, looking like she wants to murder me for a minute—probably because I winked at her in front of her kid, who promptly interrupts.

"Okay, now we all do a picture and we ask a nice stranger to take it for us. Hawk, get your camera ready." He wiggles against my front and tugs Lucy in.

A middle-aged woman passing by smiles and says, "Can I take a picture for you three?"

Lucy starts to shake her head in protest but I reach out and hand her my phone. "Thank you so much," I tell her, dropping a hand on Wyatt's shoulder and nuzzling close to Lucy. I bump her shoulder with mine. "You better smile for posterity."

"There," the woman says, beaming. "I took a few. Enjoy your evening!"

"You, too," I tell her, smiling at the shot. It's awesome, the three of us looking cozy. Like a family, I think, before I remember that we aren't. Lucy sighs as Wyatt starts looking around for the ice cream place.

"Can I text you a copy?" I have her number from when she came to my drunken rescue last night and you better believe I saved that shit.

"Maybe if you buy me a cone." She nudges me with her shoulder, seeming to accept that I'm not going to let up when it comes to her.

I grin. "Hell, Lucy, I'll even spring for rainbow sprinkles."

CHAPTER EIGHTEEN
Lucy

Kioko gives us all off on Mondays when the team plays a weekend match. I consider keeping Wyatt home with me, but then I imagine the luxury of doing our laundry and running errands by myself and I drop him at daycare. On my own, I finish all the boring chores before ten in the morning.

And then I have no idea what to do with myself. Truth be told, I really need the time alone to think. It's very rare that I get a day off while he has daycare. I decide this is what people must be talking about when they say "self care." I'm not really a bubble bath kind of person and I don't yet have the spare funds for a massage or a pedicure. My paychecks from the Forge are significantly higher than they were from the gym, but I need to save up first month's rent, last month, and a security deposit on a new place if I ever want to move Wyatt into a home that's bigger than a few hundred square feet.

Right now, all my spare funds go toward Erika's lawyer fees and all my spare energy is apparently reserved for trying to figure out my feelings for Hawk Moyer. I should probably use today to call one of the counselors Erika recommended.

I groan and change into workout clothes. I go for a run instead, enjoying the quiet of my neighborhood on a sunny day. Autumn is coming quickly, and I smile, thinking about how nice it was to bring Wyatt with me to the evening Forge game with the leaves changing colors. Mt. Washington is a beautiful backdrop for the Forge stadium.

Mt. Washington. God, what was that on Saturday night? I've spent way too many minutes staring at the picture Hawk texted me of our ride up for ice cream. I'd be lying if I said I wasn't shocked that he would rather spend time hanging out with us and sightseeing than going out with the guys.

I shouldn't be enjoying spending time with Hawk at all. I don't have time for this sort of thinking. I pick up my pace, running harder, jumping over the cracks in the uneven sidewalks. I remind myself that any second now, Erika could call with new information I have to combat from Nick or his parents. I'm sure it's just a matter of time before they figure out a way to present this current job as unsuitable and try to finagle Wyatt away from me. Or weaponize this friendship I'm building with one of the players.

Because, even though I know it's a bad idea, I enjoy spending time with Hawk. I enjoy his flirting, his innuendos, and the way he seems to *want* me. Feeling wanted that way thrills me. Maybe because I know it's dangerous.

I remember how Hawk stripped off his shirt after Saturday's goal and I pick up my pace again, trying to erase the fantasies of him naked. But the thoughts won't leave.

I think about his hands on me the night I met him, as we kissed, how gentle he felt, but also assertive, hard, making me tingle with pleasure. With relaxation. *I was relaxed on the Incline, too. Remember how he looked helping Wyatt choose an ice cream flavor?* My thoughts are traitorous, taking me down a path I'm not ready for.

I shouldn't be having lewd thoughts about one of the players on my team, or wistful thoughts, either. I head back to my apartment to clean up, my mind still lingering on Hawk. I take a deep breath as I turn on the hot water, tell myself it's okay for me to want to be wanted. I just need to want someone not-from-work. Then I remember how devastating Hawk looks when he winks at me. And he always seems to be winking.

It feels like I'm crossing a line, but as the water from my shower hits my nipples and they strain painfully at the contact, I realize there's no denying my attraction to him. What would it feel like to act on that? To seize a day of hot sex with no time constraints...for a few hours, anyway...

He called me a milf when he was drunk. I blush at the memory and then I think again about the first time, the night I met him. He would have taken me home that night, I know it. He would have fucked me, and it would have been amazing. Would I even know how to do it? How to seduce a man or respond to his advances? *Only one way to find out.* The thought makes me gasp, like half of my subconscious is challenging the other half. And damn it, I know which half I want to win.

I step out of the shower and towel off quickly, dripping on the rug in my studio apartment, biting my lip as I search for my phone. Logically, I know this is a terrible idea, scrolling through my contacts until I find his number. But I'm so attracted to him, and it doesn't seem to be going away, no matter how often I tell myself I need to stay away from Hawk Moyer.

When was the last time someone else gave me an orgasm? Maybe not since I was pregnant with Wyatt. That's pathetic, I decide, and I pick up the phone.

I pull up the contact for Hawk. *Hey,* I type.

Three dots appear on the screen almost immediately, and Hawk's reply comes through. *Lucy the task master? And just what might you want with me on my day off? I'm still sore from the last session you put us through.*

I decide to just go for it. I'm in too deep now to go back so I might as well get some enjoyment. Something just for me. ***What if I want you to make me sore, too?***

The phone rings in my hand. Hawk. "Hello?"

"Are you fucking with me, Lucy, or are you actually calling for sex?"

I shrug, then realize he can't see me. I clear my throat. "I'm looking for something casual today," I tell him. "I don't want any complications."

There's a pause and I can hear him breathing. "So…you were bored and looking to fuck someone on your day off and you called me?"

"Yes," I respond right away. "Are you interested or what?"

"Text me your address and I'll be there in fifteen seconds," he says, his breathing coming a little faster now.

"No, I can't have you over here. I'll be at your place soon."

It takes me less than five minutes to drive to Hawk's place. I park on the street and only pay the meter for two hours. If casual sex takes longer than that, I decide it's worth the ticket.

I step up to the door to buzz for Hawk's apartment, but someone coming out of the building holds the door open for me, so I step through. I bite my lip as I make my way up the steps and look for his door. My hand doesn't shake as I knock.

He's someone I work with, not just a random jock I met out with Tawnya. He's also someone I've confided in, someone who's shared a little of his own pain with me. And he's hot as fuck and…I can't help myself.

I straighten my spine and push back my shoulders. I try to find the confidence to be sexy and forget all of it when Hawk answers the door in gray sweats and nothing else. "Lucy Nelson," he drawls, eying me up and down. "Here for casual sex."

I nod. "That's right. Still feeling up to it?" I arch a brow at him and he laughs.

"You gonna blow your whistle at me throughout?" He steps toward me, and gestures for me to walk into his apartment. As soon as I'm past the threshold, he leans past me to shut the door. He's so close, and my heart starts racing. This is so outside my norm. I don't even recognize myself as I reach out a hand to touch him. Not to squeeze his arm or smack him like I sometimes do if he's being cheeky at practice.

I trace a finger along his pec, staring into his dark eyes as I feel the smooth heat of his skin beneath my hand. Suddenly, he grabs my wrist and leans close, his mouth a hair away from my ear. "What do you want, Lucy?"

I can feel his chest rise and fall with his breath under both our hands. I move to back away from him and he steps with me until I'm pressed against the door, his bare skin pressed against my t-shirt. I feel my nipples harden as he leans against me. "I don't want to make any decisions," I whisper. "I don't want to have to think about anything."

"Mmm," he says, his voice low and deep, his mouth still a millimeter away from my skin but not touching me. He's just holding me there against the door. "You want me to ravage you?"

"God, yes," I moan, and then I yelp as he steps back, tugging me toward him and lifting me so that he's carrying me through his apartment. Hawk kicks open his bedroom door and tosses me on the bed, where I bounce a few times before he's on me like, well, a hawk.

My breath comes fast as he juts his hips against mine. He's hard beneath the sweats and it feels so damn good against my needy core. Even if we just dry hump it will be worth the risk of texting him and driving over here.

But it's not going to stop at this. Hawk's mouth drops to my breast, sucking my nipple into his plump lips through the fabric of my bra and my shirt. When he moves to the other side, the wet cotton feels cool in the air conditioned room and my nipple tightens impossibly harder. I moan, digging my fingers into the muscles of his back.

He thrusts his hips again and I feel like I might come just from this touching, just from his mouth on my nipples and a few hip bumps. I start writhing on the sheets and Hawk pulls back, resting his weight on his straightened arms and smirking at me. "You need it bad, don't you, Lucy?"

"God, yes, okay? Please quit dicking around and fuck me already."

CHAPTER NINETEEN
Hawk

I've wanted this every second since the first night I met her. Now that I know more about her, how she's the one forged from iron will, I want her even more. It might make me a twisted fucker, but I even liked taking her kid out for ice cream. The more I know about her, the more I want to bite her neck and claim her as my own.

The thought is confusing to me. I've never wanted anyone like this. Each time I'm with a woman, I struggle to overcome the niggling anxiety that I'll get her pregnant. It's only a passing flicker of concern for me with Lucy. All I can focus on is making her feel good.

I take my time peeling off Lucy's clothes even as her hands are needy, trying to rip my sweats off. She palms my stomach, skirting around my cock. "You checking me for that bloat you predicted?" I wink at her and she groans. Lucy is wild for me, and that turns me on so much I feel like a savage animal.

"Hawk," she moans beneath me. "Please."

I lightly press into her sternum with the heel of my hand so she leans back and I hover over her, savoring the view of her flushed face and gorgeous tits, which are full and soft and so silky I could drown in them. Instead, I lick them. Every inch of both breasts, and Lucy likes it. Oh, she likes it. "Hawk, my

God, your tongue," she chokes out as I swirl it around the tip of one nipple, now cherry-red from the attention I've been giving it.

Her stomach skin is practically white, in stark contrast to the tan arms I've been staring at on the field each day. I bite down on her nipple and Lucy moans and writhes as I hold her hips still with one of my hands. While she's screaming and rolling her pelvis, I lean back and strip out of my sweats so that I'm naked when I nestle back between her thighs.

Lucy's hands are flailing, in my hair, scratching along my shoulders. I have a strong urge to tie her up, but she's begging me to take her now, so I'll have to save that move for another day. My dick is standing straight up against my stomach, so hard for her. I reach down and give it a tug and her eyes follow the motion of my hand. She must like what she sees, because she shoots out her little pink tongue and licks her lips, watching me tug myself. "You ready for this, Lucy?" She nods her head. "I can't hear you, baby. What is it you want?"

She beckons for me to come closer, crooking an index finger at me as she grins. When I stretch back up her body, near her face, she whispers with an emphasized Pittsburgh accent. "I want your cock, Hawk."

I laugh, loving the way she says my name. "I'm not ready to fuck you just yet, Lucy. Not yet." I rock back on my heels, grinning at her. She reaches for me and I shake my head. "No," I say. "I need to taste you first. Make sure you're ready for me."

I'm a big guy with proportional parts. I know she seems wet and willing for me, but I have to be certain. If I only get one shot at this, I want it to feel so good we both see stars. I wrap a hand around Lucy's calf, stroking her leg with my thumb as I position her foot over my shoulder.

"Oh, God, Hawk. I wasn't expecting you to—shit! Fuck! Yes!" Lucy wriggles beneath me as I slide a finger inside her.

She's so wet, so tight, pulsing around me. I quickly grab her other foot and toss it over my shoulder before I bend down and worship at the altar of her pussy. I part her curls with my fingers and slide my tongue along her slit.

I lap at her, tasting the salty tang of her arousal until she feels like a spring about to burst. I love the sound of my name on her lips, for once not in anger or ordering me around on the field. Instead, she's murmuring in ecstasy as I lick and tease her. Already, I can tell when she's getting close and because I'm a cocky prick, I back off right before she comes, rubbing along her thighs instead before going back. I could edge her all day, but eventually she digs both her hands into my hair and pulls my head up so I'm looking at her face.

"Hawk Moyer. If you don't make me come I'm going to kick you in the ears."

I grin and laugh. "As you wish," I say, before diving in for one final lick. I give her clit a pinch and slide two fingers inside her as Lucy detonates. She falls to pieces on my bed and her legs fall limp from my shoulders. I feel her clamping down around my fingers and I hold them inside her until the waves subside. Until she's calm and sated but still hungry for my cock.

I reach over her into the night stand and grab a condom, making sure to check the expiration date on the wrapper before I rip it open and roll it on. "You're very fastidious about that process," Lucy murmurs, one of her hands lazily rubbing her own nipple.

I nod. "Yeah, well, I don't want to initiate any unexpected babies," I say, shrugging. Fully sheathed, I crawl back up her body, nipping at her skin as I go. Without another word, I notch myself at her entrance and look into her eyes as I slide inside her. Lucy's pupils explode as I sink home. Fuck, she feels good. I take a minute to savor the feeling of being inside a woman again. Of being inside this particular woman.

But then Lucy starts topping me from the bottom, moving

her hips and digging her heels into the mattress so she can thrust up and grind herself against my pelvis. "It's like that, is it?" She doesn't even answer me, just closes her eyes and nods as she fucks herself on my cock. I pull out and she groans until I flip her over on her stomach and pat her ass.

"Shoulders on the bed, ass up, honey." She doesn't respond quickly enough so I lever an arm beneath her and haul her ass high. I run my palms over her skin, squeezing and kneading while I realign myself. This time, when I sink inside her, she keens like an animal. "Yeah, it's deep this way." I grunt as I thrust inside her. "You feel really fucking good, Lucy."

"Mmm, I'm dying," she moans. I pick up the pace. Lucy starts snapping her hips back to meet mine and the sound of our bodies slapping together echoes through my barely-furnished bedroom. I give her ass a smack and she yelps, then starts moaning as I keep my palm there, rubbing her while I continue to drill into her from behind.

"God, this is amazing," I growl, overcome by the sensations. Lucy feels so fucking perfect wrapped around me, so wet and hot and god, she's so into this. It's amazing watching her move, hearing her moans. It's not long before I feel a buzzing through my body and I know I'm close. I need her to come again before I lose it. I need to see if I can get her there another time. I start to ask her what she needs, and then I remember she told me she needed to not make any decisions right now. "Lucy, come for me," I hiss. I curl my body over her back while I thrust, feeling all that smooth skin along my front.

Lucy moans and squeezes me with her inner muscles. She tries to move her hand between her legs, to touch herself, so I beat her to the punch. I slide a hand around her waist, rubbing my thumb knuckle against her clit. Then, Lucy grabs my hand and sets the pace as I rub her in tight, quick circles. "Holy shit," I whisper, so turned on by her right now.

I feel her come before I hear her scream. "Hawk! God, yes.

Yes. Oh, oh oooooh." And then I don't hear anything else because I let out a roar and blast into the condom, over and over, pulsing inside her as she collapses onto the bed.

I pull out and fall down next to her, arm draped over her warm body, and we're both still, breathing heavy, staring into each other's eyes. I should say something, tell her how profound that was, how I feel so connected to her right now.

But she looks away, and I feel her withdrawing from me, from the intense experience we just shared. She slithers out of my arms, gathering her hair up and looking around for her clothes. "This was a mistake. It's not…we can't do this, Hawk."

And just like that, our amazing afternoon feels hollow.

I feel really exposed all of a sudden, and I sit up and reach for a pillow, tucking it over my crotch as I watch her yank on her clothes. "Why the hell not? Plenty of people work together and manage to have relationships."

"Ha." She picks up my pants and throws them aside as she looks for her panties. "Hawk, you were there in your kitchen while I told you about the nightmare that is my personal life. I don't have space for a relationship. I just wanted…" She drifts off and sighs.

"You just wanted to get fucked," I spit out. "You were very clear about that, Lucy." I press my lips together. "Maybe you should find someone else the next time you feel that urge."

She stands with her hands on her hips. "I'm sorry, Hawk. I can't do this. I'll see you at work."

She walks stiffly out of my apartment and I lie in my bed, staring at the ceiling, taking stock of my situation.

Pros: I reached a salary goal, I play professional soccer, and I live two hours from my mom. Cons: My head is fucked, I've got a whole secret family I'm not ready to deal with and … I caught feelings for a woman who only wants me for my cock.

I should call Josh or Reggie and open up to them. They've

been pushing me to be real with them, to build that off field connection so we can strengthen our mojo on the field. But what am I supposed to do, call them and say I had a banging booty call and am sad she left me naked with my dick in my hand?

I can't really call my mom about this. It's not like I can call my brothers... fuck. I have brothers. I have three fucking brothers. "Fuck!" I shout and throw a pillow across the room. I sit up and drag my hands down my cheeks. I peel off the soggy condom. It lands in the trash with a plop and I stare at it, feeling exactly like it looks.

CHAPTER TWENTY

Lucy

I sit in my car and stare out the window for a long time after I leave Hawk's apartment. Thankfully I do not have a parking ticket. I laugh at the absurdity of thinking of that at a time like this. I don't know what the hell is wrong with me. I crossed a line and had sex with a colleague. Is he a colleague? My subordinate? I laugh again at the thought of Hawk being anyone's subordinate. Either way, he should be off limits.

Impulsive, fun shit is for people without baggage. I have to be "on" all the time, to keep my job and to keep my kid and to stay safe. I can't afford this sort of diversion. What did I just jeopardize for an afternoon in Hawk's arms? *God, maybe it was worth it...*

I drag my hands down my cheeks as I think about the risk to my job, let alone the risk to the fragile shell of a heart that's somehow still beating inside my chest. That was hands down the most intense sexual experience of my life. Hawk is such an intuitive lover. He can read my body so well. And I just left him in there! I walked away from him like he's nothing.

I groan, thinking of all that I know about his history, and how I probably played into his insecurities by walking away. He told me to find someone else to fuck next time I feel horny. As if there could ever be anyone else after that.

He certainly doesn't need me messing with his already-fragile head space, especially when he's dealing with all his family stuff. I hate that I sent him such mixed signals today. It's not fair to him and I owe him an apology. Of course, I'd need to talk to him to offer that, and I know that talking to him will lead me to picturing him naked. Gah!

I check my phone in an attempt to distract myself and I almost faint in relief when I see an email from the Phe-Moms asking if anyone is up for a quick game of pickup this afternoon. Many women on the team are teachers or professors—at least eight people chime in that they're available.

Eager for the distraction, I add my name to the "in" list and hurry home to grab my cleats. When I get to the field, my teammate Dina shouts and waves from the turf. "Lucy! We need to establish a presence. It's every group for themselves with no permits today!"

The park is crowded, with people playing pickle ball and running hurdles on the track. There's even a group of folks clad in all black, dancing through a Tai Chi sequence under the trees behind the far goal. In the middle of this bustle, I spy groups of athletes eyeballing the open field, hoping to snag it for their own activity. The Phe-Moms are often fighting to claim space, even when we do have the permit. It's a pretty strong metaphor for most of my adult life.

At least once a week, someone tries to boot us or just infiltrate our game. Dina gestures to a group of frisbee players looking to use the turf, too, so I hurry over to her and lay out some cones. We trade some long passes, successfully claiming a slice of field until more of the Phe-Moms arrive and I lose myself in the energy and sounds of a pickup game in a busy urban park. Surely I should be able to compartmentalize my life like we did for this field? We've got multiple, distinct groups co-existing here and everything seems to be flowing pretty smoothly.

I try to shake off what happened earlier. I made one slip up and gave in to my lust. Just once. Maybe if I play hard enough, I can somehow erase the feeling of Hawk's hands on my skin. I realize my thoughts are scattered and I'm not making any sense. This is definitely reflected in my play.

At one point, I charge after the ball, growling as Patty swerves in front of me and manages to steal it away, kicking it down field toward Soma, who scores. Frustrated, I shout, "Shit!" I stomp my foot, angry that my lack of focus cost my side a goal.

"Hey," Patty says, signaling for a water break. "What's up, Lucy? It's not like you to get heated." She's right, of course. Part of the vibe of the Phe-Moms is that we're all here for fun, to challenge each other in a positive way.

I lean my head on Patty's shoulder. "I'm sorry," I tell her. "I should just view it as a growth opportunity when you get the ball away from me."

"That's the spirit," Patty says, giving my arm a squeeze.

I try harder to focus on the game. I've got about one hour left before I have to pick up Wyatt. One hour of time to do what I always do with the Phe-Moms: shut out the stress of the world and just focus on soccer.

But today, it doesn't work. I keep seeing Hawk's face as he worshipped me with his body, the way his eyes conveyed a tenderness that shook me to my core. Because if I respond, if I open myself up to receiving that kind of emotion...

I choke down a sob as I think about how easily I lost myself in Nick. How quickly things moved from him sweeping me off my feet to him ruining my life. I can't do that to myself again. I can't do that to Wyatt.

I have so much in my life to feel thankful for right now. I've got these women around me, probably wishing I were paying better attention to our soccer game. I've got a kick-ass job I need to keep. I need to keep my nose to the grind stone.

Hawk Moyer will find someone else without baggage,

though the thought of him with another woman curdles my stomach. I steel myself to block a kick and it bounces off my shoulder just as Soma shouts that we're done for the day.

I smile at Patty as I reach for my water bottle. "Sorry I was a mess today."

"No worries. That's the beauty of a team sport, right? There are always other people on the field in support." I close my eyes, wishing I could confide in her, not sure what's holding me back.

Patty is quiet, like she's waiting for me to say more. Suddenly I feel ashamed of how I behaved earlier, of how I let it bleed into the game this afternoon. I don't say anything, shifting my weight from foot to foot as I pull off my cleats. Eventually, Patty asks, "You off to grab my buddy Wyatt?" I nod and she grins. "Tell him She-Ra says hey."

My heart warms as I imagine delivering the message. My life is full right now, thanks to Patty and the Phe-Moms. I can get past this infatuation with Hawk. I owe him the space to focus on his game, on connecting with his brothers.

I, likewise, need to focus on soccer *and* on work. I need to box up whatever feelings I'm having toward Hawk and forget this afternoon ever happened. "This is the way," I mutter, quoting Wyatt's new favorite show.

CHAPTER TWENTY-ONE
Hawk

The next day I decide to come in a bit early and stop by Lucy's office. I know her shit is complicated, but I also know that yesterday wasn't a freak of nature sort of thing. We have a connection, damn it. I wasn't alone in feeling that. I knock on her door frame and push the door open. "Hey, Lucy, can I talk to you—oh."

She pops her head up from her desk and I see that she's got her kid on her lap. "Hey, Hawk."

"Hawk Moyerrrrrrrrrrr," he shouts, imitating the stadium announcer when I scored a goal the other day.

I laugh. "Hey, bud. You joining the team?"

Lucy kisses the top of his head. "Today is the day Kioko takes the twins and Wyatt to the Science Center. Isn't that so nice?"

I nod. "It's amazing."

She looks up at me and her face shifts. "Can I do anything for you? We've got a little time before practice so Wyatt is just hanging out."

I bite my lip. "I, uh, wondered if you had my training plan for this week. For conditioning and weights and…"

She raises a brow at me. "Did you check your locker? I put everyone's plan in their locker this morning."

I nod. "Right. Sorry. I stopped here first. I'll go check…"

God, she's really serious about shutting me out emotionally. She said no strings. She's got a kid. What am I even doing?

I have no idea, but something takes over my body and causes my mouth to speak the words, "Wyatt, you want to come along and see the locker room?" She grimaces and I realize it's a shitty ploy on my part so that I can see Lucy again when I bring Wyatt back. I groan inwardly at myself, but Wyatt springs up and reaches for my hand. "We're holding hands?"

He nods his head and flexes his fingers. I give him one of my fingers to cling on to and walk down the hall with him, appreciating the sticky warmth of his hand wrapped around mine. He babbles on about some show he watched on TV, and all I can think is *what sort of asshole gives up on their chance to be a dad?*

Of course my training plan is sitting in my locker right on top of my folded uniform. I show Wyatt around the room and he asks me, "Are we gonna see any guys' butts?"

A laugh bursts out of me. "I sure hope not! These guys have stinky, hairy butts." He roars with laughter. "Let me walk you back to your mom, okay?"

"What if we run?"

I nod. "Get set…"

He dashes ahead of me down the hall, yelling, "Go!" And I pretend to hurry after him. He dives into Lucy's office in a fit of giggles, saying he beat me. It feels good to be chill with this kid. He seems to like me, and I like that. I like how I can talk to him without thinking too hard about what I'm going to say. Like it's natural to just joke around with Lucy's son.

Kioko pokes his head in and asks if he's ready to go, and he's up like a flash. Lucy bends down to kiss him and thanks Kioko, smiling wistfully as they walk away. "You're great with him," I tell her, hoping the compliment sits well with her. I mean it. She seems at ease, like she has a really strong connection with him. And her love for him is obvious.

She turns to look at me and bites her lip. "You're great with him, too. Which is super odd because you're a prickly thorn to everyone else!"

I shrug. "What can I say? I like kids. I don't like adults." I grin at her.

She tilts her head, considering. "Why's that?"

I lean back against her office door. "Kids are honest," I tell her. "They tell it like it is. They usually do what they say they're going to do."

Lucy tugs on her ponytail, running her fingers through the chestnut strands, making me wish I could wrap that hair around my wrist and yank her head back and bite her throat again.

"Why'd you really stop by here, Hawk?"

I swallow. "I just…wanted to talk about yesterday."

She nods slowly. "Yesterday was terrific. And now that's done and we're at work."

I stare at her, trying to tell whether she's being truthful. I don't see any flicker of doubt in her expression, so I take a deep breath. "You're joking, right?"

"Pardon me?"

"We're well beyond *just terrific*, Lucy."

"Hawk, this conversation cannot happen here and it shouldn't happen at all."

I take a step forward and put my hands on the desk. "It's already happening. It was happening when you came over to check on me and it was happening when you called me to get fucked. We—" I gesture between us. "We are happening, Lucy. What's so wrong about that?"

Her eyes flash and her face turns red with emotion. She leans closer to me, her voice low. "I know you probably didn't get a chance to look at your plan yet. This is probably a conversation best had with Todd, but here we are."

I glare at her. "Out with it."

She takes a deep breath. "Okay, well, everyone's general

consensus is that your current barriers to improvement are, well…" Lucy bites her lip, like she's considering. "Mental."

"Mental?"

She nods. "Yes."

"Excuse me?"

Her eyes flash. "Your situation with your paternity is impacting your performance. You told Coach as much."

"You've been discussing my personal life with Coach?" This is unreal. I told him that shit in confidence and I told her things in confidence. That doesn't give either of them the right to sit and converse about me behind my back. "I didn't hear Coach complaining after the Baltimore game. I think I've got my shit in check." I stand and take a step back from her desk, crossing my arms over my chest. The woman who texted me for a booty call yesterday is sitting here talking to me about my mental health?

She closes her eyes, like she's counting to ten. "Hawk, it is my job to analyze these aspects of your performance. Which is why it is inappropriate for us to engage in any sort of relationship outside of the team. Period."

I shake my head. "No. This is bullshit. You like me, Lucy Nelson. You like spending time with me and you feel good when you tell me things. This isn't about my 'paternity situation' at all." I use finger quotes to emphasize her words right back to her. "This is 100% about you being afraid to trust anyone."

She throws her hands in the air. "Hawk, I will own that it was inappropriate of me to call you yesterday. But you've been working pretty hard to get in my pants, too. We can both be grownups and move past casual sex."

"What the hell is that supposed to mean? I've been nothing but patient with you and you just want to keep me as some secret side piece you can fuck when you're bored." I shove my hands in my pockets so she won't see me flexing and opening my fists in frustration.

She looks like she wants to slap me. "You understand that this job means everything to me, right? You know you're not ever getting fired here and I'm the one with everything to lose? And I've got a child to feed? I know you understand that part, because you told me about your life as a teenaged roofer, Hawk."

Shit. I forgot I told her about that when I got drunk. I stare at her and her eyelid tics. She's right. I've got nothing to lose here and she's risking her livelihood to get freaky with me. I should apologize, but I'm way too heated to be a good guy right now. I march out of her office before either one of us says anything else we might regret.

CHAPTER TWENTY-TWO

Lucy

After Hawk storms out of my office, I feel like I want to punch someone. But of course that's not an option. So much for my plan to compartmentalize. Where's Wyatt's Mandolorian when I need him to bring me a helmet I can hide behind?

I said some shitty things to Hawk, but I have to keep him distant. I cannot let something like yesterday happen again. Christ, what if Nick's parents were to find out I slept with someone from work? I can only imagine the motions they'd file in family court about my loose morals.

I recall my vow to become a person who does things, rather than waits around while shit happens. I stare at the sheet of counselors in my desk drawer, but I still can't imagine making that kind of commitment. I recall some of the services at the women's center, that they have support groups for women who have fled domestic violence.

When I first left, I decided those groups weren't for me because Nick had never physically harmed me or Wyatt. The court-issued no contact order and pending child endangerment charges remind me otherwise, and I pull up the website for the group. I see that they have a meeting next week with free childcare provided. I grit my teeth, RSVP as a yes and then storm down the hall to the supply closet.

Inventory seems like the perfect task for this afternoon, methodical work that can distract me from everything that happened today. It's been on my list of places to explore but I have been scared to go in there in case the previous coach peed in there, too. Or worse.

My fears are in vain, however. I open the door to find heaps of new-in-box equipment I can use to torture the Forge for hours. I actually clap my hands when I find a box full of resistance parachutes, momentarily forgetting the fight I just had with a man I'm trying not to care about.

A few of the guys come upon me in the hall as I line up all of the new gadgets I found and I hear them groaning when I hold up agility ladders to detangle. "Ha," I say, eyes bright. "Tomorrow is going to be amazing."

"What if a few of us just make this disappear on you, coach?" Reggie acts like he's going to drop a box of resistance bands into the trash.

Coach Todd chuckles as he makes his way down the hall toward his office. "I think Coach Lucy would just use her expense account to order some new shit. Ain't that right, Lucy?" He snaps his gum and grins.

Apparently I have an expense account. I stand up from the treasure trove and grin. "I don't need equipment to torture you with," I tell them. "But I'm sure gonna make use of what we've got here." I spend another hour making note of everything in the closet before retreating to my office to adjust my plans for tomorrow's fitness sessions. I have to figure out the right approach to inquire after that expense account Coach Todd mentioned.

I'm very aware of my position as temporary seat filler in this role. I don't want to come across as someone who spends frivolously, but I also don't want the management to think I don't properly utilize resources.

I scour my work email for the word "budget" but come up empty. I keep thinking of Kioko's comment when I first met him, about how the team was gathering for alcoholic drinks in season. I suppose the staff is aware that the players imbibe occasionally, but I'd really like to get a nutritionist in here to refine a plan for the athletes. It's barely October. We can still make a difference by the time playoffs begin in earnest.

Chewing my pen, I dial up to the management office, hoping to catch an admin. "Nina speaking. How may I direct your call?"

"Oh, great. Nina, this is Lucy Nelson from downstairs. Could I bother you for some help?"

"You bet," she quips. And she sounds cheerful enough, so I go ahead and ask her both how much is in my expense account and how I access it to do things like hire vendors to help with the team. The number she spits back at me is truly staggering and I hang up the phone shaking my head in disbelief. I often forget how much money there is in professional sports.

I immediately call one of the sports nutritionists I used to work with years ago at Pittsburgh University and she refers me to someone who's able to consult right away. I squeal after I hang up, knowing that tomorrow will not only be a day full of fitness fun, but will also begin a total dietary overhaul for half the guys.

Tomorrow will bring entirely new opportunity to shine in my job. I growl at the memory of Hawk suggesting I'll never get past Nick enough to trust anyone. Just because I don't want to dive into something more serious with my subordinate at work doesn't mean I'm permanently damaged by my psycho ex.

I told Hawk I wanted no strings. He's the one who pushed for more, pursued me. I just want to focus on keeping my job and keeping my son safe. I had to go and complicate everything and initiate something physical. It feels like a sacrilege to contain what Hawk and I shared to "something physical." But I can't very well sit around and pontificate about how we shared a spiritual experience.

I've turned my life around in so many ways, and today is just the next opportunity to prove it to the staff here. I deserve this job permanently and I know that I'm going to take the team to the next level.

The Forge crush Philadelphia on Friday night and I feel a spring in my step about it. The guys looked great and Coach Todd gives me a hug when he see them fooling around chugging water after the game. "They're not even reaching for the hard stuff, Lucy." He shoots his famous finger guns at me and I laugh, hugging myself.

On a rare weekend without a soccer match, I take Wyatt to a pumpkin patch along with Tawnya and her boys, the five of us lounging on a hay ride eating apples as if we don't have a care in the world.

That feeling slips away early Monday when Hawk spends the entire morning glaring at me. He's dismissive in the weight room, gruff in the afternoon stretching session and flat-out ignores me on Tuesday. As I rush to pick up Wyatt after practice, I decide it's probably for the best.

This is what I asked of him, to leave me alone. Keep things professional at work. Wyatt and I eat sandwiches in the car as I hurry from his daycare to the women's center for the support group. Of course, he gets jelly all over the front of his shirt and I'm not sure why, but the sight of it sends me right over the edge.

As I pull into the parking spot, I stare at his shirt and his sticky face, and I just start sobbing. I don't even know why. Work is going great. Erika thinks my case is going great. I'm doing what needs to be done. I'm even outside a fucking support group where I'm probably the least abused person, yet here I stand sobbing.

Wyatt looks up at me from his car seat and starts crying, too. "I'm sorry, Mommy," he wails. I climb into the back seat and unbuckle him, pulling him into my lap. I sit there rocking him, both of us sticky with peanut butter and jelly, and I cry as I watch the other women and their children file into the building. "Great," I mutter. Now I'm also going to be late for the damn meeting.

I take a deep breath and fish around for some wipes, cleaning us up as best I can, and I walk inside, preparing to make excuses for our appearance and our lateness. But as soon as I open the door, we are greeted by smiling, excited staff members. As they take Wyatt's information and walk him to the play room, I find their kindness to also be overwhelming, and I start crying again.

Eventually, someone guides me into a seat and hands me a box of tissues, which I sit and clutch as the group gets going. A few women share highlights of their week—familiar themes like making it to daycare drop off on time and managing to get to the grocery store so they don't have to rely on takeout. I actually whoop along with the crowd when one of the women smiles and informs the room that she showered every single day since she was last here. Maybe I'm not so out of place here, after all.

The next morning, I'm determined to accept the atmosphere at work, which is that Hawk grows increasingly distant while the other players and staff seem more and more at ease with me. I remind myself that Hawk is feeling hurt and vulnerable about his personal life on top of my rejection. This will all sort itself out and hopefully I'll still be working here when he's ready to be friendly again.

I wait for Coach Todd's signal that the locker room is all clear—I'd asked him to just text me or something but he insists on poking his head into the hall every morning to shout "dicks are covered!"

I walk into the room smiling bright. "Who's ready for the Lucy Gauntlet?" I ask, rubbing my palms together. They eye me skeptically, especially Hawk, who seems broodier than ever. Good. I'll give him something to brood about. I gesture for them to follow me onto the field, and I break them up into four groups. "We're going to do intervals. I've got battling ropes, resistance parachutes, agility ladders, and plain old sprints for you all to run today."

More groans. I cackle. "You think Hartford is sitting around eating greasy fries? I watched their game tape, fellas. We've got to be agile and ready to change directions. Hence…" I spread an arm toward my creations. I count them off by fours and set them through 90 second work periods with just 20 second of rest. We go for 10 rounds before our goalie starts puking. Coach Todd raises an eyebrow at me so I whistle for them to take a break.

"But don't go anywhere," I shout to them. "Phase two of the gauntlet is on her way out here right now." They collapse on the grass inside the penalty box as Piper the nutritionist emerges from the entry gate, right on time. I let them rest for a few minutes while I greet her with a high five.

"Hey," she says, looking around. "This is amazing."

"I know! I can't wait to hear how they're doing with the nutrition stuff."

She wags her eyebrows at me as Coach Todd makes his way over. "Todd," I say, "Meet Piper Conklin. She's the one who drew up the nutrition plans I sent around."

He beams. "Terrific to hear, Lucy. We need all the help you can get us, Ms. Conklin."

"Piper, please," she grins and shakes his hand. "I'm ready to strip these men of all their bad food habits."

I let her get her papers organized as I call the guys in to stretch. "All right," I tell them. "We've got another round on the gauntlet, but while you're recovering and stretching your hammies, I need to introduce you to the next secret weapon we've got for you."

I pause in my pacing when I feel Hawk's gaze burning into

me. He and most of the guys have stripped their shirts by now. Of course, they're all fit and firm and glistening with sweat. But only Hawk catches my eye as he bends over, the muscles of his back flexing while he reaches for his toes. I remind myself my interest right now is purely chemical. He brought me orgasms, he looks amazing, and my synapses are just firing accordingly.

He's also angry and in a messed up head space about his family situation. I have no time or space to lend him my spare thoughts. I stand by while Piper talks the team through the general basics of the nutrition plan, asking them about the timing of their meals, how they're doing with the new recommendations. "I've got binders for each of you in your lockers," she says. "We'll start with some general guidelines this first week until I can meet with you individually to refine the plan." She grins and slaps me on the back. "Between me and Lucy, we're going to shed every ounce of lethargy off of you. By playoffs, you're going to be peaking, in top form, feeling like a million bucks."

"Yeah, but only some of us are earning that much," Reggie jokes, shoving Hawk in the shoulder. It should be a good thing, the guys teasing him. The team chuckles but Hawk doesn't smile. He just continues to glare at me, and I still feel the burn of his anger at my rejection as I blow the whistle and send them through another round of torture.

CHAPTER TWENTY-THREE
Hawk

I feel like shit, and it's not related to my diet. It's also not related to the ramped up physical torture Lucy has been putting us through the past few weeks.

My mood is 100 per cent related to my fucked up family situation and my love life. Exactly what I screamed at Lucy for suggesting. She's absolutely right that the thing I need to do most is sort out my feelings about my father, but so far I haven't even called my brother back.

Tim texted me that he's got an inside source at *The Post* who is keeping the story hushed until the Stag family works out a response. He included me in that phrase. The Stag family. I haven't even met any of them apart from Tim.

I'm not speaking to my mom right now, either. I'm pretty much just going balls out every day at practice and then holing up in my apartment with canned tuna and my own misery. No Lucy. No family. The more I circle around it, the more I feel angry that I yelled at this woman who's just trying to mind her own business and keep her job.

I know I owe her an apology but I also don't know how to go about doing that in a way that doesn't further jeopardize her situation here at work. The longer I go without talking to her, the bigger it all seems. I don't fucking know how to talk to women. I've always been focused on soccer, unless I was focused on bringing in more money for me and my mom. Relationships always just seemed like a distraction.

I can't figure out why it bothers me that this woman is everything I say I want. She's hot, she's fantastic in bed, and she doesn't want anything from me apart from my cock. So why is it I fall asleep each night thinking about her laugh?

Yesterday at practice, she worked us to the bone. And in the afternoon team session, we played better. As a team, we were cohesive. Sharp. We all feel immediate effects from Lucy's work, and even if she took away all our ice cream and burgers until further notice, she's definitely earned the respect of every man on this field.

And that? That's irresistible to me.

I'm supposed to be working the battling ropes again this morning, two massive black ropes I'm supposed to thump on the ground and shake until my abs feel like they'll tear. But all I can do is stare at her as she helps Reggie to fasten the resistance parachute around his waist.

I hear her telling him this will help his acceleration, make him better able to burst onto a pass when it's headed to space. And I know she's not having a sexual response to wrapping her arms around him to buckle the chute. But as I growl at the ropes all I can think about is the feel of her nipples against his back and that it should be me receiving all her touches.

In another world, where she wasn't terrified, she'd be rubbed up against me, helping me train, kissing me when I have a good game. But this isn't another world and the woman who should be mine…can't be.

Fuck. Lucy doesn't need someone else going caveman on her, acting possessive. That's the opposite of what she needs. I need to hone my focus on this impossible workout. Burn the lust right out of my body.

But then she walks near me and picks up that fucking whistle and puts it between her plump lips. I stare as she purses her mouth and gets ready to blow. And I damn near come in my pants. Fuck.

When Coach announces we're ready for cooldown, I throw the ropes on the ground and sprint to the locker room. I can't fucking deal with "gentle stretches" today. I'm too worked up. I march directly to the showers, throwing my clothes on the ground in my wake. I'll pick them up before the team manager comes for the laundry. I need to calm down.

I blast the water on full pressure and stand there, steaming under the hot spray.

"Hawk!" Shit. I hear her voice even in here, where the steam of the shower is supposed to drown out my reactions.

"Hawk, I'm talking to you. You need to cool down properly—you can't just storm off the field. They're having a meeting out there!" I whip my head around the glass partition of the showers and I see Lucy standing in the locker rooms with her hands on her hips. The water pelts down on me as I stare at her and her eyes narrow in on my dick, standing straight up against my stomach now. My nostrils flare as she looks.

I press a palm to the glass and bring my other hand to my cock, and give it one hard pull. And then Lucy licks her lips and I'm on her, pressing her back against a row of lockers with a crash. Her breath whooshes out before I press my lips to hers. Her fingers slide into my wet hair and I nip at her neck, looking down as my wet skin soaks her gold Forge t-shirt.

"Hawk," she breathes. "Someone could come in here."

"Let them fucking see, Lucy. Look how bad I want you." I bring her hand to my cock and she groans, her hips jutting forward. "I'll fuck you so fast, Lucy. You'll come so hard." She licks my collar bone and she must taste the sweat there. I feel her hand dig into my ass, her fingers kneading the sore muscles.

I reach for the waistband of her shorts, sliding a hand inside and finding her wet. She gasps as I trace a finger along her seam. "Let me make you come again, Lucy." My breath is hot on her cheek and I resist the urge to yank her ponytail and drag her into the shower. I trace her clit with my finger, feeling her squirm.

I want her to scream my name. I want to bite into her neck and mark her as mine. My lips meet hers in a fierce collision and her moans erupt into my mouth. She's close, so close, and I'm so turned on by the sight of her, wet from touching me, wrecked by my touch. I grab her thigh with one hand and hoist her leg up around my hip. "Look how good we are together, Lucy. Fuck, I need you."

Suddenly Lucy stiffens and she pulls her head back. I don't know what I said, but the moment is gone. I can feel it in the air around her as much as her posture. I back away and she ducks out from under my arm, damp from the water on my body.

She shakes her head, her lip trembling. I reach for her but pause, my hand in the air. "What do you want from me, Hawk? You told me to call someone else when I feel horny. You want me to sleep over? Hold you? Because you know damn well that can never happen. I've got enough demands on my affection." She spins on her heel and reaches for a towel on the cart by the showers. She throws it against my chest. "Pick up your shit when you're done."

CHAPTER TWENTY-FOUR

Lucy

What the hell am I doing?

I rush from the locker room like it's on fire, my head spinning. Hawk seemed so angry as he glowered at me all this week. I thought I only followed him into the locker room to check in. I should have turned around and left when I saw that he was naked.

I should have.

Why does it have to feel so fucking good to be with him? God, he's right. About all of it. I want him, badly.

But if I give in to that urge, I stand to lose everything.

Again.

And I have so much more now than I had the first time I had to start from scratch with Wyatt.

Jesus, that kiss. His naked, wet body pressing me against the lockers. Holy shit, that was hot.

For the next two days, I can think of nothing else. I try to resist touching myself to thoughts of Hawk, naked and ferocious, wanting me. It's not fair to him.

I'm like an addict, and my drug of choice is Hawk Moyer. It

doesn't help that my son wants to wear his autographed Forge jersey every day and ask me when his buddy will take him out for ice cream again. Despite a few sleepless nights agonizing over the new drama I created, that I didn't have time for, I manage to lead the team through an uneventful training session and guide them through a long stretch after film.

I—just barely—manage not to make eye contact with Hawk at all during work hours. I also don't call him and I don't offer that apology that I definitely owe him.

We're away this weekend, against New York.

Kioko and Todd said I can bring Wyatt along for away matches and that it's fine, but I know it isn't. Kioko's got Tawnya at home handling things while he travels with the team. Everyone else at work is professional, focused only on the game. I can't meet Wyatt's needs and see to the team's needs at the same time. Even if I felt okay being the only parent passing out applesauce on the sideline, I literally could not keep Wyatt safe while keeping my eyes on the action on the field.

I seem to be the only one upset about dropping Wyatt with Tawnya as an alternative to bringing him. She springs out her front door, waving excitedly when I pull in the driveway early Saturday morning.

"Wyatt, guess what?" She squats down low to help get him out of his carseat as I grab his bag from the trunk.

"What?" He wiggles in anticipation.

"We're gonna take stuff to build a blanket fort on the sidelines at a bonus Phe-Mom practice today. Isn't that awesome?"

He claps his hands and runs into the house where the twins are waiting to whisk him away to their room.

"He didn't kiss me goodbye," I pout, looking after him wistfully, wondering if I should chase him down for a hug.

Tawnya drapes an arm around my shoulders. "Did he sleep

with you in bed last night?" I nod, wondering where she's headed with that question. "Then I am pretty sure you got plenty of snuggles in to last him until you fly back."

I laugh and shake my head. "Got me there." I used to feel touched out when Wyatt needed me close all the time, but now that he's at daycare and I've got work, it's sort of nice to reconnect with him. I'm also excited about taking a business trip right now, though. And that feels foreign to me.

"It's so strange to me that I'm going somewhere on a plane. I can't tell you the last time I went on a trip." I hand her Wyatt's bag and she hefts it over one shoulder.

"Well I personally think you should let Wyatt stay overnight. I know you want to totally minimize the amount of seconds you think you're putting me out, but it's better for all of us if he just stays over and you come join us for pancakes tomorrow morning." She gives me a knowing look. "Think of it this way. Your flight gets in around bedtime. I'd have to keep *all* the kids up late if you're going to retrieve him from me."

I bite my lip. "Are you sure?"

She puts a hand on her hip at this. "Do I ever say things I'm not sure about?" She flicks me in the shoulder. "Besides, maybe this gives you space for a little more self care this evening. You can go out on the town. Live a little."

I laugh. "Out on the town! With who?"

"Oh, maybe the other Phe-Moms? I hear they go out dancing from time to time." Tawnya sighs and glances up at the house, where the three boys are pressed against the glass in the twins' bedroom window, making little pig snouts with their noses. "Look, Lucy, all I'm saying is I know you carry a lot of tension and your life has a lot of challenges. If keeping Wyatt overnight here gives you space to go out and find some ease…" She shrugs.

I think about Tawnya's words as I drive to the stadium. I think back to the support group, where I didn't say a word but listened as nine other women talked about wrestling with the same sort of guilt I have, about relying too much on friends for childcare and struggling to focus on their work while they're at work.

It's not my work that's got me feeling uneasy, though.

I climb aboard the bus and consciously don't look at Hawk. I force myself not to think about him as I sigh at my emails from my custody lawyer, who says Nick's parents are trying to argue they should have visitation with Wyatt even though Nick is living with them and we have a no-contact order in place.

I have no business getting involved with Hawk to find ease or anything else, not with all that going on in my life. And yet, he does make me feel good.

I think about Tawnya encouraging me to find joy while I guide the team through their pre-game warmup, while I watch them shut out New York 2-0 with Hawk scoring one of those goals.

In the locker room, after the match, the team is jubilant. We've clinched a playoff spot and a first-round bye, with home field advantage for the second round.

Everyone is hugging everyone and a few of the guys try to lift Todd in the air before I yell at them not to strain their backs. Reggie and Josh squeeze Hawk and he grins. This is the first time I've seen him really gel with his teammates, really enjoy himself.

The defensive players stand on the bench, singing an old British song about a juggler with large balls and Hawk's face lights up. He climbs up and joins them, as do a few of the other players who are from other countries, or at least spent time playing soccer abroad. Soon, half the team are standing on the bench in their cleats, singing and swaying and making me nervous they'll slip and hurt themselves.

"Coach!" Reggie reaches out to me, distracting me. "Did

you see my speed? I'm faster than Hawkeye's flashy car." He and some of the offensive players embrace me, and I don't even mind the sweat as they do.

"I saw," I say, patting Reggie on the shoulder. "All of you looked great." Hawk catches my eye and his smile shifts to another expression, this one heated and sultry. I clear my throat and run my fingers through my hair. "I'm going to step into the hall so you can all clean up." I clasp my hands together. "Amazing work, everyone."

I lean against the wall in the hall outside the locker room, smiling at the media and the few scattered fans making their way out of the building. I grin as I see Kioko approaching, his arms held wide.

"Lucy! My secret weapon!" I return his friendly embrace and he stands next to me, leaning against the wall. "I have to thank you," he says. "Not only do you provide my sons with the best playmate in the entire world, but then you come and join my staff and make these Forge players look like the superstars we all knew they could be."

I'm not sure what to say in response to such praise. My first instinct is to deflect and say something about how I couldn't possibly have done all that much, but I think about my history with this work. I'm a good coach. I was damn good at my work at the university and even at the gym, I was always able to help my clients reach and exceed their own goals. "Thank you," I say to Kioko. I meet his dark eyes. "I really hope I can continue to build on this progress."

Kioko chuckles. "Why on earth would things be otherwise?" I hear his phone chirp and he reaches into his pocket. "Ah! Look at this!" He shows me a picture Tawnya sent. Our three boys are huddled into the bottom bunk in the twins' room wearing matching pajamas with the Forge crest. "All is well," he says. And I agree.

After our flight lands in Pittsburgh, and we all climb in the team bus, I get my own chirp text message. This one from Hawk. ***Can we talk?***

I feel a rush of heat in my belly at the thought, and before I can second guess myself, I respond with a yes.

We get back to the stadium and I take my time in my office, listening as the players grab their things and file out to the parking lot. I hear them making plans for the evening, joking around. I hear their voices fade and finally I hear nothing but a quiet tap on my door frame. I look up to find Hawk standing there, arms crossed, gaze heated. "Want to go for a drive?"

I nod and when he gestures his head to leave, I follow him. He walks toward his car, gleaming under the lights in the parking lot, and opens the passenger door. I slide inside, running my hands along the leather interior.

He climbs in and snaps on the radio, and I smile when I hear the local independent radio station pumping out bluegrass. "I never picked you for a hillbilly."

He grins. "You like it," he says, glancing over at me when he stops at a light. "You like a lot of things about me, Lucy." I close my eyes and bite my lip. I nod.

CHAPTER TWENTY-FIVE
Hawk

"Where are you going?" She furrows her brow when I put on my blinker to turn right at the light near my apartment instead of left. I grin.

"I still don't have any furniture," I tell her. "I was hoping you could help me pick out some stuff."

Her eyes widen and then her entire body relaxes. She grins. "Are we going to West Elm?"

"Does West Elm sell couches?"

She smacks my chest. "Are they even open this late?"

"They better be." Lucy purses her lips and moves to get out her phone.

"I checked! I checked. We have til ten. And I'll need every second." I shrug as she laughs. "People usually do that shit for me."

Lucy rolls her eyes. "West Elm sells very expensive couches. And coffee tables. And night stands." She pokes me with her index finger and then looks toward the store, considering as I park.

I don't want her to run off again. I don't know why. Yes I do, damn it. I like her. I like that she's thorough and organized and good at coaching. I like that she's helping the guys improve their soccer skills by opening up their hip joints or whatever the hell she says her exercises do for us.

"Come help me pick stuff out," I tell her. I bring her hand up to my mouth and kiss her knuckles.

"I don't know." She sighs.

"Come on. It'll take a half hour. Then when we get my new couch back home, I can..."

Lucy roars with laughter, her head dropping back, her throat moving as she laughs. "Just what I always wanted! Couch sex."

I wink at her. "I promise I'll make it worth your while." She sighs. "I'm just teasing, Lucy. I could take you out for a drink after. Or make you some tea." She gives a tiny nod, and I know I've got her. Two minutes later, we're breezing through West Elm with a sales clerk hot on our heels.

I try to hold Lucy's hand, but she shakes herself loose from my grasp and I remind myself that I can't push her too far or she'll leave. I point to a living room display. "Do I want leather furniture, Lucy? It says it's timeless."

She shakes her head. "You'll get sweaty and your thighs will stick to it."

I grin. "Wouldn't want sticky thighs." Everything I'm saying to her is an innuendo and she knows it. She blushes while she steers us toward a thick, plush sofa.

"This one is nice," she says. "And it's on sale."

"Whatever the lady thinks," I say to the clerk, who has an electronic tablet where she's checking stock or some shit. "Can you deliver this tonight?"

"Oh." The clerk seems surprised. "Well, I'd have to check our stock room…"

"We want the floor model," I tell her. I hand her my black Am-Ex card and her eyes widen. "We're going to pick out a bunch of shit and I'll pay whatever for you to bring it across the street when we check out."

Lucy stands with her mouth hanging open, making eyes with the sales clerk. Lucy shrugs. I smile. "You said I need a coffee table, too?"

The clerk taps a finger on her lip and studies me. "Do I know you from somewhere?"

Lucy initially grins that I'm being recognized, but then shirks back, as if she's scared she'll get noticed too. I want to tell her there's really not too much chance of that, since I know it makes her nervous, but she's already wandered away to where they have the bedroom models set up.

A few minutes later, Lucy has picked out a cushioned headboard for me as well as a bunch of pieces of furniture. Everything comes with human first names like Anton and Parker and I tease her about it while I wait to get rung up. "Are you going to start naming your drills after guys on the team? Tell me the really shitty workouts will be named Todd."

Tucked behind a column, Lucy must feel confident nobody can see us or else she's just gotten more comfortable, because she swats at my chest again but smiles at me like she's warming up to the idea of hanging out with me where people can see.

"So." I put my hands in my pockets and lean a shoulder on the wall near her. "Couch tea or bar beer. Is that a thing?"

"Bar beer...I don't think it sounds like a thing." She bites her lip. "Can we do the tea?" She gestures around the shopping plaza. The stores are closing but the restaurants and bars are hopping, with football on the huge TV screen and a live band getting set up out in the courtyard.

"Sure," I tell her. "It would be hard to hear each other talk out here, anyway." I drive us across the street with the delivery truck right behind us. I slip the guys a few fifties from my wallet and they get my shit set up faster than I can pour Lucy some herbal tea.

She perches on a stool in my kitchen while I see the crew out of my house and lock the door behind them. I flop backward onto my new couch, which smells slightly like plastic wrap and air freshener. "What do you think now,

Lucy? More settled?"

She sips her drink and spins around to stare at me. "It's a big difference."

"You should come see it from this angle." I pat the cushions next to me. She laughs and shakes her head. I feel a surge of joy when she sets her tea on the counter and walks over to the couch. She squeals when I tug her toward me and pull her in, wrapping my arms around her. I run my fingers through her hair and I wait for her to talk to me. When she doesn't, I ask, "How did you meet him, anyway?"

I feel her shrug in my arms. "He was working on something electrical at the stadium, where I was training the college players. I caught his eye." I stiffen as she tells me he was charming at first, how he bought her things and seemed so eager for her attention. I try not to draw similarities to my own pursuit of Lucy, knowing her story is about to take a dark turn. I feel her swallow. "Eventually I realized the attentiveness was jealousy, and then the jealousy began to feel scary. But I was pregnant and had left my job and sold my car. Hawk, I was totally reliant on him."

Her voice is quiet, almost a whisper. "I think he cut holes in the condoms. We always used condoms. I don't have any way to prove that. And I don't regret Wyatt."

"Of course you don't." I kiss the top of her head and squeeze her tight. I see how her son lights up her world. And I know because my own mother has always told me how much it meant to her to be my mother.

"I have implants now," she says. "For birth control. I asked for them at my checkup after Wyatt was born. The doctor just puts them in my arm. I wanted to be in control of my body. I wanted it to be my conscious choice, you know?"

I can't help but laugh at that revelation. "You saw how I am with condoms. Trust me, Lucy, I get it."

We're silent as we fall asleep and I just hold her, and she lets me.

CHAPTER TWENTY-SIX
Hawk

I arrange to meet my brothers at Tim's house. His wife and kids went out with...I forget which brother's wife and kids. Or maybe they're all together, talking about us. I'm not ready to meet the whole crew just yet. I'm on edge just at the idea of this.

He told me to be here at 6, which left me with an awkward time gap after training. I try unsuccessfully not to fill it with thoughts of Lucy, so eventually I park down the block from Tim's address and call my mom. There's been tension between us lately, ever since I told her what happened with the reporter. I'm still feeling a lot of big, conflicting emotions about missing 26 years of bonding time with my brothers.

"Hey," I say when she picks up the phone.

"Hi, honey," she says. I hear a commotion in the background.

"Oh, crap, are you at work?"

"It's okay. I'm on my break." I can hear beeping skid steers and people shouting about crates of milk. I always hope my mother will go get a cushier job now that I bought her a house and paid off the mortgage, maybe at a spa or something, but she insists she likes her Grocer Joe family.

I sigh. "I just wanted to tell you I...well I was talking to someone with a shitty ex. She's a single mom. Anyway, she gave me some things to think about. Like from your perspective."

"I appreciate that, Hawk. I'm sorry that I kept you in the dark, as you say." I clear my throat. I don't want to fight with her today. She takes a deep breath. "I was talking to my sponsor about what happened. How you found out about your father from a reporter."

I perk up at this. "I don't think I knew you still have a sponsor, Ma."

She laughs. "I'll always have a sponsor, Hawk. That's how it works when you're an addict." There's a pause and I hear her moving around. "Baby, I've been letting my shame about my past take precedence over your pain. I let that reporter embarrass you by keeping you in the dark." She starts audibly crying and I feel my body tingling with strong emotions.

"Ma, I…" What do I say to her in response to this? I can't say it's okay, because it's not. "I appreciate you saying that," I tell her, finally. And then I change the subject. Sort of. "I'm meeting my brothers today. In twenty minutes."

"You are? Wow."

I can't think of anything to say to her after that. I think about Lucy pointing out that I can still have a future with them, that we can have a relationship, my brothers and me. But it's not that easy to shake off the sadness that I spent years not knowing they existed.

"Hawk, I know you wish I'd contacted him, that I'd reached out, that you could have grown up with family connections."

"Ma, I—"

"But Hawk! What if he came for you? What if he tried to take you from me? You have to understand that I am an addict in recovery. A teen mom. Jesus, Hawk, do you know you're my higher power?"

"What do you mean?"

"You," she says, and I hear her sniff through tears. "You

are my thing. My focus. My sobriety meaning. When I was pregnant, I found the purpose I lacked. God, you were my miracle, baby. I couldn't risk losing you. If I didn't have you here, needing me every day, I'm certain I would have slipped back into that darkness, Hawk. I know it."

"I didn't realize any of that, Ma."

She draws a shuddering breath. "I know. I worked real hard to keep all that ugliness from you. But it's part of you, too. And now you're a grown man. And I'm really glad you have this chance to make some connections."

"Ma, I don't want to put your sobriety at risk."

"Oh, that's not what I meant by telling you all that." I hear her blow her nose. "I just…I guess I just wanted to explain, that's all. What I was thinking then, in not telling you earlier."

"I used to hear you crying, Ma." My voice is almost a whisper as I confess to her.

"Oh, baby, I had no idea. But I wasn't crying because I wished Ted Stag would come into our lives and help. It was just hard, that's all. It would have been hard no matter what." She laughs. "Kids are hard!"

"So I've heard," I mutter. In the rear view mirror, I see a bunch of kids spill out of Tim's house and a curly haired woman loads them all into a silver Volvo. I watch as she backs out of the driveway and drives away. "Hey, Ma, I'm sorry to cut out like this. I gotta go…"

"What are their names? Your brothers?"

"Timber, Tyrion, and Thatcher," I tell her. She repeats them back to me. "We're hanging out at Tim's house."

"Well, enjoy yourself, Hawk. Send me a picture?"

"A picture?"

"Yeah." Her voice is lighter now. "You should do a selfie. Capture the moment. The four brothers Stag meet at last…"

"We'll see, Ma. I love you."

144

We hang up and I climb out of the car, locking it as I make my way toward Tim's house. The door flies open as I raise my hand to knock. A huge man who resembles Tim opens the door and holds his arms out wide. "Are you him? Of course you're him. You look just like us. Except for the eyes." He leans forward and pulls me in by my shirt sleeves, wrapping his arms around me. "Hey, Thatch, I think he smells like a Stag."

I hear a voice say, "How's that, Tyrion? Mountain air, fresh cedar, and salt lick?"

I peer around the shoulder of the man who is hugging me, presumably Ty Stag.

"No," he says, sniffing me again. "Old Spice." He looks at me. "Do you use Krakengard?"

I see Tim standing at his kitchen counter looking stern and another man with long hair and a beard, sitting on a stool with his arms crossed. I push back from the hug and straighten out my shirt. "Nah. ," I say. "Swagger."

Ty's face light's up. "See? I told you guys! Swagger all around. They might as well call it Stag Brothers. Oh, I'm Ty. Bet you figured that out. I used to be the youngest."

I raise a brow at him. "Let's hope I stay the youngest, right?"

All three of them laugh at that and Ty slaps me on the back, ushering me toward the counter. We're silent for awhile, Thatcher tapping his fingers on the marble surface. I give a little inhale through my nose, finding an odd sense of happiness when I recognize that all the men in this room are indeed wearing the same deodorant. Tim eventually slides me a glass of water and I raise it to him in thanks. "So," I say, awkwardly. "Did he, um, say anything? About me? Or my mom?"

"Who? Dad?" Thatcher grunts. "He mostly got pale and sank into a chair. We called his sponsor and haven't really talked to him since."

I watch Tim swallow before he says, "Dad's been sober for about five years now. Six?"

"Five," Thatcher confirms. "Since Petey's first birthday." They all nod.

"This is awkward as hell," Ty says, pacing around the room. "And we can't even get shit faced together because Hawkeye probably has a diet plan or some shit."

"Please don't call me that." I hate when my agent makes Marvel references, even if he says he's just alluding to my deceptive left-footed accuracy.

Thatcher snorts. "Get used to it, man. Ty has a nickname for everyone."

"You love it, Thatchy," Ty says, dropping a kiss on his brother's cheek and making a move to ruffle his hair. Thatcher elbows him in the throat. Tim and I stand there staring at them both.

"So," Tim says, nodding toward the pair, now wrestling on the tile floor. "Welcome to the family I guess."

I met my brothers today. I text Lucy as soon as I get home. After she came over last night, I decided I'm not going to push her to define anything, but I'm also not going to hold back anymore. Not when it comes to her. To us.

I send her the "ussie" Ty took, his long arm holding the phone as he squished the three of us in against him. There are some benefits to being tall, not that the rest of us Stag brothers are short.

My phone rings in my hand a minute later. Lucy. "You all look so much alike," she chirps. "Are they nice? I mean, Tim is…stern…"

I laugh. "Yeah," I tell her. "They're nice. Kind of a pain in the ass already. They demanded VIP seats for the next Forge game."

"They can sit in the owners box, right?"

I tell her how they have nine sons between them, and it

takes her a minute to recover from thinking about all that testosterone. "So many fart jokes," she mutters.

"Ha. Yeah." It feels right to talk to Lucy like this. I know it puts her on edge any time I try to point out that we're connecting, so I just enjoy the moment, sharing with her. "Did you have soccer tonight?"

"Mm hm. I scored a goal."

"Bad ass," I say, imagining what she looked like in her shorts, maybe a tank top, running up and down the field. I try to conjure some sexy *Baywatch* fantasy of her running, but when I picture it, I just see her as fierce and powerful. Which is also sexy. Shit, now I'm hard. "I wish I could have seen that."

"You should come watch sometime," she says quickly. And then she gives a little gasp.

"Too late to take it back," I tease. "You already made the invite."

"Kioko comes sometimes, to get the boys from Tawnya."

"You'd think they'd hire someone to help or something."

"Nah," Lucy says. "They like the boys to see Tawnya in her element. I like it, too. When Wyatt watches me play. He thinks my team is as good as yours." She laughs softly and I imagine her looking at her sleeping son with a smile on her face. I used to wake up sometimes and see my mom sitting on my bed, smiling at me, rubbing my feet through the covers.

"I'm sure the Phe-moms are amazing," I tell her, smiling.

"You remembered the name?"

"I remember everything you tell me, Lucy." She's quiet for a bit and I wonder what she's thinking. But I feel like I pushed her far enough for one night, so I tell her, "I'll see you tomorrow morning."

"Night, Hawk."

We hang up and I stare at the second pillow in my bed, leaning in close to inhale the scent of her hair, still hanging around my apartment like it's meant to be here.

CHAPTER TWENTY-SEVEN
Lucy

I'm starting to get careless, but I can't seem to stop. Hawk keeps sneaking into my office to grope my ass or kiss my neck and...I let him. More than let him, I lean into his touches and spend way too much time thinking about the next time I can get away from Wyatt and from work to get naked with Hawk.

So when he texts me to take my time leaving work on Thursday, I do. I wrap things up slowly, listening as the team files out of the stadium toward the parking lot. I hear the loud steps of Coach Todd exiting the building along with his assistants. And then I hear the whisper of my door hinges.

I look up to see Hawk standing there, dark and disheveled, his cheeks pink from his workout, or maybe the heat of his shower. Or maybe both. I rise from my desk silently, and in an instant I'm in his arms, the door to my office closed as he presses his mouth into mine.

He moans softly against me and leans me against the edge of my desk. "God, you feel good, Lucy," he whispers. We kiss and nibble at each other, my hands pressing into his shoulders as his explore my body through my clothes. I don't know how long we spend making out, but I know it has to end. I pull my mouth from his and rest my forehead against Hawk's.

"I have to go get Wyatt," I say. "But this was nice."

"Just nice?" He pinches my thigh and I squeak in response, then blush.

"More than nice," I tell him and I reach up to kiss him near his ear, in the place that I know makes him shudder. And the fact that I know that tells me I'm in way too deep. Well past fuck buddies. "Hawk."

He leans back and grabs my hand. "I know," he says, and walks to the door, pulling it open. "I'll walk you to the parking lot. You got your stuff?"

I nod and fall in step beside him, pressed against his arm, savoring the nearness of him. The gentle, friendly silence we have together. Hawk pushes open the door for me and I brush against him as I pass, teasing him by rubbing my chest against him. He walks out the door and reaches for my hair, but I see something catch the afternoon sunlight and draw my eye.

I freeze.

Nick is in the parking lot of the stadium. I see the hateful look on his face for an instant before I duck behind Hawk, panting, breathless. I peek around his shoulder and see no sign of Nick, but he was there. I know that he was. This is very, very bad.

My breaths come quickly as I struggle to regain control of my body. I've never responded this way to seeing him before. *Terror,* I think. *I am terrified.* I close my eyes, and then scream as I feel myself being moved.

I open my eyes to see Hawk gently backing me to the building, his eyes dark with concern. "Lucy," he whispers, his thumbs gently rubbing my arms. "Lucy, what's wrong?"

I can't speak. What is Nick doing here? I mean, obviously he's spying on me or trying to intimidate me or both. But what are the logistics of him being here? I have a PFA against him.

"Lucy!" Hawk's voice is thick with worry and my eyes

flash wide. "You're shaking, honey."

I look down at my hands. They are indeed shaking. "Nick," I manage to say as Hawk stares intently into my eyes. "My ex."

Hawk clenches his jaw and whips his head around. "Where? He's HERE? What the fuck, Lucy?"

I press my hands into my jeans, trying to think. Erika was very clear that if Nick violates his no-contact order I have to call the police, because if I don't he might be able to tell a judge that he doesn't pose a threat to me. "I have to call the police," I say, but my hands are shaking too badly to pull out my phone.

Hawk is in front of me in an instant. He squeezes my hand and pulls out his own phone. The 911 dispatch operator patches him through to zone 4 precinct, where my paperwork is filed. I swallow and feel a tear slip down my cheek. Nobody there ever takes me seriously. Maybe Hawk will carry more authority...

"No," he says, his deep voice stern. "This isn't a *simple custody dispute*. I'm telling you a dangerous man is—it doesn't fucking matter if I'm 'the boyfriend.' He's breaking the law and it's your job to enforce this!"

I swallow again, imagining the conversation on the other end of the phone. I remember the first time Nick showed up at the gym when I was working and the reporting officer said he couldn't do anything about a "lovers quarrel."

Hawk holds his hand over the phone and whispers, "They're checking his location...Hello? Yes, I'm here...Well I'm sure he is back at his residence *now*...what do you mean he's entitled to data privacy? You're not going to check where he was an hour ago? What the fuck are you all doing over—" Hawk stares at the phone in his hand. "They hung up," he says. "They said they'd make a note and they fucking hung up."

I nod, and take a breath. "I have to get Wyatt." I swing my

purse around to my hip and start striding toward my car. Hawk places a hand on my arm.

"Honey, you cannot drive like this. Look at you. You can barely hold the keys." He's right. I'm fumbling, struggling to press the button to unlock the doors to my car. I start to cry.

"I have to get my son," I shriek, my voice high pitched with terror. Hawk pulls me against his chest and wraps his arms around me. I squirm, my body desperate to get moving. Get to Wyatt. "I have to get to him, Hawk. Before Nick…"

Hawk nods and plucks the keys from my hand. "I'm driving you," he says.

I shake my head. "No, Wyatt's car seat. I need…"

"Shh." He walks around the passenger side and opens the door. "I'm driving you in your car, okay? And I'm going in with you to grab Wyatt." My jaw drops in shock and gratitude, but I sink into the seat, unable to think of a valid protest to his suggestion. All I can think about right now is Wyatt.

Hawk climbs in the driver seat and slides the seat all the way back, adjusting the mirrors to accommodate his height. He looks like a giant in my tiny Civic. I try to make a mental note to tease him about it later, but I can't seem to find the words to do it now. I grip the interior until my knuckles turn white.

"Lucy, tell me where to go, honey."

"What?"

"What daycare is Wyatt at? Do you have an address?"

"Oh." I pull out my phone and pull up the daycare in the map app. The bluetooth in my car picks up the phone and I relax a bit when the computerized voice says we will be at our destination in twelve minutes.

I remind myself that Nick doesn't know which daycare Wyatt attends. Things will be okay for 12 minutes. They have to. "This will be okay," I say to myself. I look down to see my legs are shaking and my fingers are twitching.

"Jesus Christ, Lucy," Hawk mutters, looking at me at a red light. "I want to kill him for whatever he did to scare you like this."

I shake my head rapidly. "It wasn't me he hurt," I whisper.

The light turns green and Hawk's eyes bulge as he squeals ahead, driving faster than ever.

CHAPTER TWENTY-EIGHT
Hawk

I can't believe this is happening. I'm racing through downtown Pittsburgh to rescue a child from his own father. I can hardly breathe, I'm so angry at this fuck for scaring Lucy and, apparently, hurting Wyatt. The kid is four years old. What sort of monster harms a child?

The same sort who abandons his family. The same sort who leaves a pregnant teenager to overdose in a homeless encampment. I grind my teeth together as we drive and I manage to shave two minutes off the predicted arrival time by weaving in and out of the lanes of traffic.

We reach the facility and I thank everyone and everything in the universe that there's a 15 minute loading zone parking space I can pull into. I leap out of the car to make sure I'm right beside Lucy, who races toward the door.

A staff member sees her coming and waves, buzzing open the door. Lucy rushes past her into the brightly-lit space and the staffer looks at me, confused. I clear my throat. "Did anyone come here asking for Wyatt?" She shakes her head. I lean on the counter. "Lucy thinks…Lucy saw her ex today and was worried…"

The woman nods sympathetically. "Ah. One of those days." She clucks her tongue. "Well we have all the relevant info on file here for Wyatt, so we would never release him to anyone not on Lucy's approval list." She eyes me up and down. "No matter how good-looking they might be."

I grin at her, appreciating the moment of levity. Just then, Lucy walks past the desk carrying Wyatt, who is wriggling and trying to get out of her arms. She has a vice grip on him. "I'm so sorry, Sheila," she says to the woman at the desk. "I just had to hold him, you know?"

"It's okay, baby. Your friend here told me the gist of things." She pats Lucy's arm and smiles at Wyatt. "We'll see you in the morning, won't we, baby?"

Wyatt nods and then sees me and grins. "Hawk Moyerrrrrrrrr." This kid cracks me up. I give him a salute. I'd offer to carry him or hold his hand if I thought Lucy would disentangle herself from her son.

"Hey, bud." I pat his leg. "You want a ride?"

"Did you bring your fancy car?"

I shake my head. "Nah, I'm driving you and your mom around in your car. I'm the chauffeur today."

He furrows his brow. "Where's your fancy car?"

Lucy is apparently concerned about this as well. "Oh, Hawk, I'm fine at this point, really. I'll drive you back to the stadium and we can—"

I hold up a hand and cut her off. "My car is fine. I'm going to drive you two home. No arguing."

She bites her lip and eventually nods. We walk outside and I try to stay out of her way as she buckles Wyatt into his seat. But her hands are still shaking. "Can I help?"

She has tears in her eyes when she looks up at me. She nods and steps to the side. "I just can't get the buckle between his legs…"

Wyatt starts wiggling to try and see what the commotion is. "My ball buckle," he says. "It buckles my balls!"

I look into the car seat and scratch at my chin. "I can see that, pal. Hey, I'm going to do my best, okay?"

"I'll help you," he says, holding one end of the buckle in

his fat little fingers. I tug it into place and only pinch myself once before it clicks.

"Hey, now!" I hold my hand up for a fist bump and Wyatt giggles as he slaps at my hand. "I'll take it," I say. I turn to Lucy. "Need me to get your ball buckle, too, or you got it under control?"

Wyatt giggles. "Mama doesn't have a ball buckle, silly!"

Lucy smiles thinly. "I'll take that, too," I whisper. I pull out onto the street and realize I don't know where she and Wyatt live. "Hey, so, I'm finally going to need that address from you." I wink at her, hoping my efforts to lighten the mood aren't too evident. I'm still mad as hell but I appreciate Wyatt being here because we both seem to need to appear calm for him.

Lucy types her address into her gps and I realize it's just a few blocks from where I live. "I didn't know you live this near me," I tell her. She nods.

"I used to work at the gym there by the taco place." She shrugs. "I wanted to live close to work."

"Makes sense." I note that her apartment is on the other side of Penn Avenue from my condo complex. I know money was tight for her and I worry we'll be driving into an unsafe neighborhood, but I start to relax when I see tidy stoops with flower pots and cheerful signs in the windows along her street.

"This is us," she says and I pull over, parallel parking her car in a tight spot. I toss an arm around Lucy's seat so I can turn around to back into the spot and I make a face at Wyatt after I back in. He loves it, but starts kicking his feet, hitting Lucy's seat. The jolts seem to scare her again and her face turns white.

I turn off the car and place a hand on her thigh. "Hey," I tell her. "I don't think you guys should stay here tonight."

She seems relieved at the suggestion and nods rapidly. "You're right," she whispers.

"Why don't I come up and help you throw some things in a bag. You and Wyatt can come back to my place for a few days, stay as long as you want. I'll order some pizza. You want pizza, bud?"

"Pizza!" Wyatt looks between me and his mother.

Lucy puts a hand on my arm. "Hawk, I really appreciate the ride. But we can't stay with you."

I furrow my brow. "Why the hell not? You're not staying here, that's for damn sure. Lucy, you're white as a sheet. I'm not letting you be alone right now."

She shakes her head. "I'll call my friend Patty," she says.

Wyatt claps his hands. "Patty! She's She-ra, Princess of power!"

I stare at Lucy. I should have figured she'd want to stay with friends. I'm reminded yet again that I'm not actually her boyfriend. We are fuck buddies. Colleagues who cuddle but don't discuss it. I drag a hand through my hair and take a deep breath. "Of course," I say. "Whatever you need. Tell me an address and I'll drop you." She opens her mouth to protest and I hold up a hand. "I'm a superstar athlete, remember? I can afford a Lyft home."

Lucy sighs and nods her head. Together we get Wyatt inside and I play with him while she runs around packing a bag. Her apartment is a tiny studio bursting at the seams with stuff for Wyatt. Lucy's own things seem to be limited to a small dresser in the corner and a closet that appears full primarily of Forge-branded clothes.

I don't think this neighborhood is so expensive that her Forge salary can't buy her a little bit more room, but I guess this isn't the time to ask her about it. Lucy drops two duffel bags by the front door and looks at me like she can't decide if she wants to carry the stuff or her kid.

I stoop to pick up the bags and, looking relieved, she picks up Wyatt. I don't stop to think about the consequences, but I reach out and stroke her cheek with my thumb, dropping a soft kiss beneath her eye. When I pull back, I see her face is wet   with   tears.

CHAPTER TWENTY-NINE

Lucy

"I can't thank you enough for letting us crash here on late notice." I follow Patty into the house after Hawk takes off, Wyatt babbling excitedly about a sleepover with She-Ra.

"It's really not a problem," Patty says. "My girls are at their other mom's house tonight, so Wyatt can have his pick between a gothic princess room or a ballerina paradise." I laugh as she gestures in the doorways of two very vibrant, very different bedrooms.

"I like the black one," he says, wriggling out of my arms to go investigate.

"I got some of my girls' old toys out of the closet for you, Wyatt," Patty says. "Check them out and come find me if you have any questions."

Wyatt's eyes bulge out of his head when he sees the huge box of blocks and play food. As soon as he's engaged, Patty nods toward the kitchen and says, "Come on. I'll make a cup of tea and you tell me what's going on."

I sink into a stool at her counter and tell her about seeing Nick in the parking lot. She frowns over the sink as she fills the kettle. Patty was subpoenaed to appear in court for Nick's upcoming trial. I hate that my drama has sucked her in like this and now I'm drawing her further into the web by asking to crash here. "I should get a hotel," I say. "Gah. Does he have access to your info as a witness?"

Patty frowns as she sets the water to boil. "I can't imagine it would be very ethical for his lawyer to share my address." She shrugs. "But who knows how ethical someone is to agree to defend a guy who locks his kid in a hot car while he goes to the bar?"

The kettle starts to boil and Patty pours two mugs of tea, walking around the counter to sit in the stool next to me. She slides me a mug and a plate of different tea bags. "Lucy, it's no trouble to have you and Wyatt sleep over." She elbows me. "You're my teammate! Wouldn't you say yes if I called looking for a place to crash?" I bite my lip and nod. Patty grins. "Someday you'll pay it forward. Hell, one of my girls might end up calling you when they decide I'm too humiliating for words."

I laugh at that. "It must be difficult to raise teen girls." I dunk my tea bag a few more times and pull it out, blowing on the hot tea before bringing the warm mug to my lips. It feels nice, comforting, just holding the mug and smelling the minty aroma wafting up around my face.

Patty smiles and shrugs. "They're good kids. And I get along well with my ex." We sip in silence together for a few minutes before she makes a face at me and raises an eyebrow. "Now tell me about the guy who dropped you off at my house."

I wave a hand. "Hawk and I are just friends," I lie. "He's on the team. The Forge."

"Hmm," Patty says. "He didn't look just friendly toward you…"

I wince. "I don't have room in my life for anything serious. I mean, look at today. I'm not exactly the best candidate for a fun relationship." I know I'm babbling, but I haven't had an opportunity to think through the emotional roller coaster of today's interactions with Hawk. Making out in my office felt so right, so fun, and so intimate. And then…he didn't even leave room for argument when he took me home, brought me here.

Patty keeps her brow raised and takes another sip of tea. "I'm not what you'd call an expert on men, but that one looked pretty interested in your welfare, Lucy."

I laugh at her joke and wave a hand at her insinuation. "He's just being nice," I insist. "I'm not in a position for more."

In the morning I insist on making breakfast for Patty. She teaches art at a nearby university and doesn't have to be on campus until ten, so she sits while I serve her an omelet and fresh coffee. She and Wyatt are engaged in a cutthroat game of thumb war by the time I get everything plated and sit down with them at the counter.

"So, Patty Haute," I say. "The professor. That makes you…"

"Professor Hot," she says, laughing.

I shake my head. "That's amazing."

"The ladies love it," she says, grinning into her coffee mug.

"Well, good for you," I say, meaning it. "Between saving lives and spreading soccer love, you're like the most amazing person in my world right now."

Patty pats my hand. "You're a terrific person, Lucy. I'm glad to have you as a friend."

I get all choked up as I gather Wyatt's and my things to get ready for our day. I was pretty isolated from friends and family by the end of my relationship with Nick. It never seemed problematic at first, the way he only wanted me to spend time with him. By the time he started accusing all my friends of poisoning my mind against him, I was fully dependent on him financially and alone in our apartment with a newborn with no car, no job, and no more friends. I still feel like I can't offer much to Patty in return for her hospitality, but she insists I bring good energy to the Phe-Moms.

"Soccer is an outlet for all of us," she says, walking me out to the car. "When you help raise the level of play, you challenge everyone there to be better. That's not nothing— that's everything, Lucy."

I wave a hand at her. "Now I'm going to cry before work."

"Well, so what? Cry and feel your feelings and have yourself a vulnerable day and we'll work it out on the field later, right?"

I nod through my tears, buckling Wyatt in his seat. "I'll see you at the field."

She pats the roof of my car and waves goodbye to Wyatt. "I'm going to block one of those left-footed goal attempts of yours one of these days, Lucy. You better not go easy on me."

CHAPTER THIRTY
Hawk

I leave Lucy and Wyatt at her friend's house and my mind is racing. I decide to walk around the block and try and calm down, take stock. I went from the most perfect kisses with her in her office to seeing her panicked and fearing for her life because she laid eyes on her garbage ex.

I stare at my phone in my hand and sit on a bench at a bus stop near Lucy's friend's house. I need to fucking vent to someone about this because I still don't even know what just happened here.

And then I remember that I have brothers. Normal people would call their brothers about something like this.

I sigh and look at the time. Almost seven. I don't want to fuck up dinner or bedtime for anyone, but I honestly have no idea what time either of those activities take place for a normal family. I decide to just call Tim since I know he knows Lucy and a little bit about her situation.

He answers after two rings, his voice muffled like he's speaking in a hurry as he leaves a room. "What's up, Hawk?"

"Hey. So." I blow out a breath and run my fingers through my hair. "Something really fucked up happened today and my head is all messed up about it." I recoil as a bus blows its horn at a car cutting it off. "Also I need a ride home."

Tim tells me to hold tight, that someone will grab me soon.

I don't have to wait very long to figure out what he means by that. A few minutes later, a gold minivan screeches to a halt by the curb and my brother Ty opens the window. "Yo, baby, climb aboard the Stag-mobile."

I pinch my lips together and walk toward the van, leaning in the front window. "How'd you know where to get me?" He beckons his hand at me when the light changes, and I hurry into the van as cars start honking at him.

He squeals away as I buckle my seatbelt. Ty turns onto a bridge—I still have no idea which ones are which—and slaps my thigh. "Timbo told me there was a Stag in need." He shrugs. "I was close by picking up June-bug's dry cleaning. You still haven't met my wife, man! She's the best."

I smile. "From what I hear, Tim and Thatcher's wives are *also* the best."

Ty grins. "Yeah, well they're all your sisters-in-law I guess, so you probably shouldn't play favorites." He winks at me. "You can have a favorite brother, though. Who picks you up from a shitty bench on the South Side, Hawky? Who? Me, that's right!" Ty pounds on the roof as we cruise through a yellow light. I can't help but feel relaxed around him. He turns to face me again and asks, "So Tim said something's eating at you. Wanna spill now or wait til we're at the park?"

"The park?"

"Oh, Tim didn't tell you? In this family, we go for long runs when we're upset. Hope you're not too tired from practice." Ty cackles and then whistles. "Just kidding, man. I know damn well you're beat. We'll go easy on you."

My eyes go wide as I realize he's serious, that he's driving me to go running with my new-found extended family. He pulls over in the one-way loop in Highland Park near a huge garden and glances at my outfit. I changed into sneakers and sweats after practice, but not necessarily sneakers I want to trash by running. "These are $400 Yeezy's," I mutter, bending forward to tie the laces tighter.

"Oh, just invoice Tim if you scuff 'em. That's what I do in these situations." Ty bends over next to me, stretching and reaching for his toes. He doesn't look like a guy who retired from pro hockey years ago. He looks like he's still training four hours every day. He's got at least four inches on me in height and probably fifty pounds of muscle. I feel like a kid beside him.

I hesitantly begin to stretch my quads and I see the dark heads of my two oldest brothers coming up Highland Avenue into the park. Is it weird that I feel calmer about the whole thing already, just being with this group of men I barely know? I haven't even told them anything yet. Maybe it's because they didn't give me shit about anything and just picked me up for a ride, no questions asked.

"Hawk," Thatcher says, giving me a nod and running his hand through his beard. I nod back at him.

Ty looks around at all of us, grinning. "This is so great, right? There are four of us! I mean, it's obviously a huge mind fuck. But also it's great!"

Tim clears his throat. "Hawk said he needs help sorting through a situation. What do we think? Three miles of conversation? Four?"

I realize he's asking me and my eyes go wide. "I, um, already had two practices today. Three I guess?" Tim nods and starts running, so I follow him. I've never been to this park before, and I take in the massive flower gardens before he makes his way around a bend. There's a wide pedestrian path marked off from the car traffic, and the whole thing seems to circle the reservoir.

We run past families picnicking, kids playing on playgrounds, and a group of teens slack lining between some of the trees before Thatcher says something. "So, the idea is, you're supposed to tell us what's bothering you and we see if we can help."

Tim frowns. "I think he knows how it works, Thatch."

These guys aren't even out of breath and we're keeping a pretty good pace. I guess I come from good cardiovascular genes. I sigh.

"So, there's a woman."

"Ah." Ty nudges me with his shoulder. "We're great at this sort of advice. You trying to woo her?"

"Maybe? It's complicated."

Thatcher shakes his head a few times. "We've got nothing but time, brother. Well...two and a half more miles of time. My wife might castrate me if I don't make it home in time for the kids' bedtime."

"Way to make him feel like an asshole, Thatch." Ty shoves his brother, making him stumble, and Thatcher tries to trip Ty. I have to jump over them to make my way over to Tim, who has stopped running while they squabble.

"As you were saying?"

Eventually, Ty and Thatcher form some sort of truce and start running again. "So, uh, I really like her. But she..." I hesitate, but remember that these guys are squeezing me in for a pep talk here. "She works with me. And she has a super fucked up situation with her ex and she stands to lose a lot if she goes out with me. But I really fucking like her. And did I mention she works with me? So I have to see her every day."

"You got a woman on the team?" Ty looks like he swallowed a mosquito as he contemplates a woman playing on a professional men's soccer team. I shake my head and fill them in on the rough outline of my interactions with Lucy.

Tim slows his stride a little bit as we near the place where we started running. He looks at Ty, who points forward to indicate we should do another lap. Tim says, "Well I have some experience with workplace romance. And I have insight into your specific workplace. I can assure you it's probably a bigger deal in your mind than it is in any sort of formal, policy sort of way."

I nod. "You know I'm talking about Lucy, right?"

He shrugs. "She seems very competent at what she does."

Ty nudges me with his shoulder again. "Tim loves competence."

"That's why he hates you so much," Thatcher says, setting off another round of shoving that passes quicker than the last time.

I brush the sweat off my forehead with my arm. "I really wanted her to let me take care of her today when she was scared of that dick. I...I don't know how to get her to choose me."

My brothers all nod, like I'm making sense somehow. Ty turns around and runs backwards a bit, looking me in the eye. "Best I can tell, you've spent like 26 years wanting to be chosen by our dad, right? And now you've got this woman making you feel a similar sort of way. *And* she's got a monster of an ex triggering all sorts of other father issues inside your heart."

My jaw opens and closes a few times, because damn! "That's pretty much exactly it, man. Wow."

Ty holds up a hand and Thatcher slaps him a high five. "I'm telling you, the three of us spend a lot of time talking through this shit." Ty tilts his head at Tim. "Tim struggles with our father, too. And I get it. It's fucking terrible."

"So why don't you look like you want to flip his car or burn down Ted's house or something?" As I list these out, the idea of vandalizing his life sounds mighty attractive right now. Ted or Lucy's ex. Or both.

Tim shakes his head and breathes out heavily through his nose. "It's not productive to be angry at Ted. It doesn't help anything."

"And yet you're still angry."

He nods. "I still am." We finish another lap around the park and Tim swerves toward the stone steps leading up to the top of the reservoir. The sun is setting now and the sky is bright orange and purple, reflecting off the still water. "But I also know deep in my bones that these guys love me. That they will choose me, every time. That even if I fall to pieces they'll come collect me and stitch me back together."

Tim stops on the path and leans against the rail, with his back to the water, the sun setting behind him. "Hawk, I want you to know that we choose you, too. You don't ever need to doubt us."

Thatcher and Ty nod and the four of us stand there along the rail, watching the sunset, not talking. I start slipping again into regret that I missed decades of this, of their counsel and their horseplay and closeness. Tim, somehow sensing where my thoughts are leading, shakes his head again. "There's a time and a place for anger, Hawk. But today, you're here with us. And tomorrow, if you need us to drag you out for another pep talk, you've got us then, too."

We're silent for a while since I don't know what to say. Eventually Ty slaps me on the back and nods toward the stairs back toward his car. "Let's get you home so Thatcher can go read Harry Potter to his rascals."

"We finished that series, Tyrion. I thought I'd start Game of Thrones with them."

Ty screeches to a halt and whips his head toward his brother. "Are you fucking with me? You're reading that out loud to little kids, man?" And Thatcher grins, because he is clearly fucking with his brother, who shares a name with clever, ruthless Tyrion Lannister.

When we get to Ty's car, Thatcher drops an arm on my shoulder. "Hawk," he says. "I'm gonna give you a hug, and then I'm going home. Sound good?"

I nod. He wraps his arms around me, and so does Ty and even eventually Tim. And damn it, I do feel better.

CHAPTER THIRTY-ONE

Lucy

I have to force myself to count to five and then let go when I drop Wyatt at daycare. If I don't back away now, I know I'll just sit here on the floor with him in my lap all day, and I can't miss work. Not only are we preparing for the playoffs, I'm also meeting with Erika to review what's going on with the custody case and she has a call in to the prosecutors for Nick's criminal proceedings.

"God, I'm a mess," I mutter as I make my way into my office, fumbling with papers and dropping my clipboard on the tile floor in the hall.

"I'd worry if you weren't." I look up to see Hawk, who squats down to help me pick up the papers. He taps the stack to neaten the pages and hands it to me, letting his fingers linger along mine as he releases the bundle.

I swallow back tears, remembering how kind he was yesterday, how committed he was to making sure Wyatt and I were safe. "Hawk, I don't know how to thank you for getting me and Wyatt to Patty's house."

He nods toward my office, seeking permission to go inside, and I follow him, closing the door behind him. I'm not sure why I think he will sit in the chair at my desk, but I draw in a breath when he gathers me into his arms. "Lucy," he says into my hair. "I want you and Wyatt to feel safe. Always." He lifts my chin with one finger and meets my gaze. "Always."

A tear slides down my cheek at his words, at the thought of a man who would say such a thing and really mean it. I close my eyes and take a breath. "I'm working on it." I squeeze the bundle of papers tighter against my chest. I haven't had a chance to read anything Erika sent. I'm not sure she expected me to. A lot of it is notes she's putting together, collections of old text messages and social media posts from Nick, which got increasingly more disturbing after I left him. I was glad when I didn't have to read over them. I just requested a paper record from my phone company and handed her the entire heap. I don't want to read over them now.

Hawk cups my cheek with his hand. "Lucy, I know you don't feel comfortable staying with me, but I want to make sure you understand that you and Wyatt are welcome. Always. My house will always be a safe place for you." I swallow and nod. He takes a breath. "But I also don't think you should stay where you are. You don't have security there and there's no easy way for you to escape if he manages to get in." I see something pulse in Hawk's throat as he clenches his jaw.

"I'm working on moving," I tell him. "I'm close to where I need to be. I just have to keep shelling out more and more in legal fees to make sure he doesn't get access to my son." Hawk's eyes flash at this, but he nods, silently. I shirk back from his arms and walk around to my desk chair. "Speaking of which, I have a lot I need to get done before training. I'm meeting my lawyer here while you guys are in film."

He perks up when I say that. "Oh. Good. I'm glad. Do you need me to be a witness or anything? Tell them what I saw?"

I shake my head rapidly. "He's on location monitoring. My lawyer says they can just check. We won't need to testify or anything."

He drags his fingers through his dark hair. "Jesus, Lucy, how do you just talk about all this so casually? You've got a criminal stalking you and you're just calmly telling me your lawyer will run a report!"

I squeeze my lips together. "I told you, Hawk. I have fucking baggage. I don't get to take time out to be enraged about this. I just pay the lawyers thousands and thousands of dollars to validate what I should have seen years ago. I let myself get fooled by his charms and I let him take over my life. Now I'm paying the price to get free." I slap the desk. "And a huge part of that process is making sure *you* and your teammates are in top shape for the game this weekend." His nostrils flare as he stands there listening to me rant. "So please go suit up and bring your best effort to the field today."

"Lucy—"

I shake my head. "I'm done having a personal discussion. I need to focus."

He steps toward the door and places a hand on the handle, turning over his shoulder to look at me. "Can you at least tell me where you'll stay tonight?"

When I don't answer him right away he heads back toward the desk and leans over it toward me. "Let me pay for you to get a hotel."

I shake my head rapidly at this suggestion. "I don't want to owe you anything."

"Jesus, Lucy, it's just money to me. It's nothing. Stay at my house and I'll go stay with my brothers. How about that?"

"I'll ask someone from my soccer team," I decide as I say it. Not Patty again. Not Tawnya. They've done too much for me already. Maybe our coach wouldn't mind taking us in for one night...

"Lucy you are so fucking stubborn. Why won't you let me help you?"

I throw a pen at him at those words. "Because," I shriek, standing up so hard my chair flies back and bounces off the wall behind my desk. "The last time I trusted a man I almost got myself and my son killed." I grab another pen and throw it. "This is why I didn't want any strings. This is why I just wanted someone to make me feel good for five minutes so I could forget about the flaming bag of shit that is my life!"

Hawk leans a hand against the door and stoops to pick up the pens, which he puts on the desk. "I'm not afraid of flaming shit, Lucy. I'm going to let you get ready for practice, but I'm not going to stop making sure you're safe." I open my mouth to yell at him again but he spins on his heel and closes the door to my office behind him.

CHAPTER THIRTY-TWO
Hawk

I can't get my mind off Lucy and her situation. At training, she appears calm and put together. To look at her, you'd never know she literally fled for her life last night. She marches up and down the sidelines explaining what we should be feeling during each stretch, telling us which muscle groups should be groaning after each bodyweight exercise. She's a legend. All the guys talk about how well she works with Coach Todd so that it doesn't even feel like a separate workout session from the skills and team drills we work on for him.

After my shower, when I know she's in her office with her lawyer, I decide to call my mom to keep myself from barging in there and butting into her business. Which of course means I'm interrupting my mother at her business, but she doesn't seem to mind. "Hey, baby," she says. I don't hear a commotion in the background so maybe she's not at work today.

"Hey, Ma."

"Aren't you still at the stadium working on your game? Should I worry about getting a mid-day call from you?"

"I just needed to hear your voice," I tell her. "I was thinking more about … our whole situation."

"Situation? Which situation would that be? There's so

many."

"Very funny, Ma. I mean I was thinking about your choice to keep our lives a secret. In Ohio."

"Ah." She makes a sound in her throat. "Is this about that woman you're interested in?" I tell her what Lucy said, how she can't trust a man after what she's been through. "She's working her tail off for that baby of hers, Hawk. I can tell you know that."

"I thought you'd say 'oh, poor thing' or something."

She puffs out a laugh. "Poor thing? From what you're telling me that crafty woman found a way to escape, got herself a job, got herself a better job, and built a friendship strong enough where she had a place to go be safe last night. Nothing poor about that."

I sigh. "God, Ma, you frame that so well. Lucy did all that stuff. She's always just fully amazing."

"So what's bothering you then, sweetheart?"

I lean my forehead against the wall in the hall where I snuck away to use the phone. "I just want to swoop in and save her. I want to do something so she trusts me. I want to help her so she'll want to be with me. God, I sound so pathetic when I put it that way."

"Hmm." My mom has been making that noise a lot lately, since I moved to Pittsburgh.

"I have more money than sense, Ma. What if I just buy her a house or something?"

"Baby, she doesn't want a man to make her feel beholden. Why do you think I keep refusing to let you buy me things?" She clucks her tongue. "She needs to build the confidence that she can thrive on her own. That's when she'll want to welcome you into her life. When it feels like a choice."

Whoosh. "Mom, that's heavy shit."

"Watch your mouth!"

"Sorry." I run a hand over my face. "I don't know how to make all that stuff happen."

"I wish I knew what to tell you, sweetheart. I'm sure it meant a lot that you helped her get to her friend's house yesterday. Where is she right now?"

I roll my eyes and spin around, slumping my back against the wall. "She's in her office with her expensive ass lawyer." A thought occurs to me and I stand up straight. "Ma, how did you afford our first apartment in Loudonville? Before you got your job at Grocer Joe's?"

"Oh!" She sounds wistful. "There was a fund at church. A special fund for people who need housing help."

As she says it, I remember Lucy saying a similar program through the shelter helped her and Wyatt get set up where they're living now. "That's amazing, Ma. Hey, I just had an idea. I gotta go make a call."

"An idea about church?"

"Nah. Hey, listen, I'll call you later. I'm meeting my brothers' wives and kids and stuff before my game this weekend."

"I wish I could be there for this one…"

"I'm not upset about it, Ma. I know you'll be cheering from work."

"They said they'd play the commentary over the loudspeaker! And put it on the television in the break room."

"Awesome. Hey, thanks, Ma. I love you."

"I love you, too."

When we hang up I see that I've got less than five minutes before I need to get into the film session. I quickly dial my agent and when he sends me to voicemail, I dial him again immediately. "Hawk? Baby? Is someone arrested?"

"Real quick, Bri. I need to give a million dollars to the housing fund at the Hope church in Loudonville in Ohio."

"What? Jesus, Hawk! Warn a guy before you just spit out something like that."

"But then I also need to create a foundation here, for legal support for women."

"Hawk, baby, is this about the sunglasses endorsements? Because I told you I could have them put a shirt on you in the ad if that was a problem."

"I don't give a fuck about my chest hair, Brian. I need this foundation set up pronto." I hang up on him and head into the film room, finally feeling like I have a proactive plan.

This time, when I drive to my brother Tim's house, I don't have to hide down the block while his family bustles out the door. Instead, I hear them a mile away as I approach. I look at the expensive watch Brian has me hawking all over the internet. Apparently the Stag family shows up early for things. The door flings open and I hear a pop sound. I duck before I'm hit in the face with a foam dart, and there's a roar from inside.

Ty appears with a kid clinging to each of his legs. He has a dart gun, mimicking Sylvester Stallone in Rambo. Then he sees me wide-eyed on the doorstep. "Oh, hey, bro." He grins. "Come on inside and meet everyone. Don't tell Tim we were using guns in the house."

I shake my head. "Wouldn't dream of it."

Ty and Thatcher line up all the kids in the hall and introduce me to my nephews Petey, Wesley, Odin, Gunnar, Alder, Stellan, Byron, Ricky and Tucker. Before I can repeat the names, the kids scatter into the back yard and someone yells at them to only hit each other with the plastic bats. I can't help but grin at the chaos.

"Okay, so, these are our wives." Ty drapes an arm around my shoulders and guides me into the kitchen, where Tim is wearing an apron and following instructions from a curly-haired woman at his side as they prep a giant salad.

"Oh, Hawk!" The woman claps her hands and runs around the counter to hug me. "I'm Alice! Tim's wife. It's amazing to meet you."

She pulls back and a redhead waves at me from nearby.

"I'm Emma. Thatcher's wife."

I feel Ty steer my body so I'm facing the woman behind the stove sautéing a bunch of chicken. "And this is the Honorable Judge Juniper Jones," he says. "My wife. The Olympian."

She rolls her eyes and hands him the spatula. "Hi, Hawk." She shakes my hand. "Sorry about him."

I grin. "I think it's great how much he loves you." I shrug. "I didn't really get to see a lot of that. My family was always just my mom."

Juniper takes a swig of her beer and grins. "Oh, I know all about that. I just had my dad and then…well you can see the family now."

I look around the kitchen. Tim has stuck his head out through the sliding door to holler at the kids to stop beating up Tucker. Tim shakes his head and sits down at the table. "Good to see you again, Hawk. Have a seat."

"Yes, please sit. Dinner is just about ready." A few seconds later, Alice has heaped chicken and salad and roasted carrots onto our plates. The smell is amazing, like citrus and savory goodness. And, strangely, it all seems in line with my diet plan.

"I can't believe I can eat all this. The entire meal…" I stare at my plate as Alice beams.

She pats my hand. "I had Tim call up the nutritionist you guys are using," she says. "I asked what the parameters are for in-season and then I consulted with Juniper to make sure everything sounded yummy."

I furrow my brow, staring at her. "Are you for real? I didn't imagine you? This is amazing. Seriously, guys, this is just so far beyond anything I expected."

Thatcher grunts and adjusts his chair. "You're family, man."

They all burst into conversation, talking over each other to make sure I understand the terrific attributes of everyone at the table. I eat my food and soak it all in, listening to them talk about supporting each other's careers and helping to overcome health crises.

Eventually, Ty points his fork at me. "You should ask my wife for advice about your whole scenario. She does a lot of family law stuff, unlike Timbo."

I arch a brow and turn to Juniper. "You see custody cases and stuff?"

She gives me a puzzled look. "Yes, but you're not worried about custody, surely? You're over 18…"

I wave a hand and laugh. "Not with Ted. No, I'm not ready to deal with him yet. I'm just thinking about a friend."

Ty gives her a brief rundown of what I told them last night. God, was it only last night where they made me go running in my Yeezy's and bare my soul to them in the park? Juniper nods, looking sympathetic and wincing when I mention that Lucy's ex showed up at the stadium looking creepy.

"Hm. Those cases are always so difficult. I hate how long they take to move through the system."

"Yeah, no shit," I say, and then I look up in horror. "I'm sorry I swore."

Thatcher laughs. "We don't give a fuck about that."

We all share a laugh, and I explain that Lucy has been spending all the money she has on her lawyer. I drift off and Tim surprises me by saying, "It sounds like Lucy shares my tendency to avoid trusting others. To accept help."

Alice squeezes his hand. "You've been doing so great, honey." He smiles at her.

I clear my throat and tell them what I asked my agent to do. "I just don't know how to convince her to become the foundation's first recipient."

Thatcher finishes his food and shoves his plate forward, sitting back in his chair and crossing his arms over his chest. "Maybe she doesn't need to," he says. He shrugs. "She's got the good job now, right? Maybe she just wants to know that the foundation exists."

I blow out a breath and stare at my water glass. "Thatcher, you make a really good point. I just hate the idea of her in that apartment while this asshole is free and roaming the streets."

Tim clears his throat. "Lucy is still with the Forge in an interim capacity. The team will make a decision about a permanent contract after the season ends." He meets my gaze. "To be frank, I don't see why they wouldn't keep her on. With a bonus. The Forge have never made playoffs before and it's their first year at the premier level...not that any of that helps with the asshole ex."

Ty scratches his chin and drapes an arm around the back of Juniper's chair. "Gosh, if only you had any connections with anyone in the position to grease the wheels of the legal system..."

Juniper winks at him and rubs his leg. "Well, I *am* on the local rowing team with a few folks from the D.A.'s office."

Ty kisses her on the forehead. "Lord even knows what you all talk about early in the morning, out on the water..."

I stare at my brothers, at this family I found, who jumped at the opportunity to make me welcome, and now to help me help someone I care about. "I don't even know what to say, guys."

Tim grunts. "Say you'll keep your nephews overnight during the off season so I can sleep past six on Sunday morning."

CHAPTER THIRTY-THREE

Lucy

Wyatt loves getting breakfast in the hotel. I can't afford to be staying here, but I also couldn't bring myself to ask anyone else from the Phe-Moms to take us in and Hawk was right—there's no way I would feel safe at my apartment right now. So here we are. Having an adventure. It's a little pathetic that our hotel room is actually bigger than our apartment.

When I get to work, I see a call coming through from Erika, and I groan, knowing it's just going to keep adding on to my tab with her. I'll feel a little better when I get a contract to stay with the Forge permanently. It has to be coming—surely they're excited about us making the playoffs like this. If I can just get that contract, I'll feel secure taking the leap to sign a lease on a bigger place.

I nod my head, feeling good about that plan as I answer the call from Erika. She sounds out of breath.

"Lucy, I have some great news for you. I'll get right to the point." I grin. "I just got off a call with the assistant district attorney who's handling Nick's criminal case. They were able to move up the motions court to Friday."

I freeze in my tracks in the hall outside my office. "Friday? Like tomorrow?"

"Yes! I don't know what that man is thinking, but he's putting in a motion to suppress the charges. I'm pretty confident this judge isn't having it, Lucy. The D.A. confirmed that he was at your workplace the other day. Huge red flag. His lawyer is claiming he was there for a job estimate. That's easily verified as false."

I bite my lip. I'm not sure how to feel about any of this. Relieved seems like the wrong emotion. "So…if this suppression thing works, what then?"

Erika sighs. "Look, that is NOT going to happen. You have a witness who rescued your little boy from a hot car. They're not going to throw those charges out, Lucy. They're just not. But if he successfully argues to suppress the charges, then…" She sighs. "Yes, if that happens he'd get off and his family would double down on the custody crap." I sink to the floor, my heart racing and my breath coming in gulps. "Lucy, I hear you panicking. I'm telling you, that is not going to be the outcome tomorrow. Your friend Patty has already been deposed. The judge has already seen all the pre-trial paperwork. This judge's wife works at the Women's Center as a pro-bono attorney for their clients. I assure you he sees through your ex and his parents and their ploys."

I'm not sure what happens the rest of the day after I hang up with Erika. I know I get a text from Patty that she's pumped to trash Nick in court. I know I walk out to the field with a whistle in my hand and I know a few hours later, I see a pile of sweaty soccer players collapsed on the field, but I have no memory of taking them through their workout.

At one point, I'm standing in the middle of my office staring at an empty whiteboard when Coach Todd clears his throat behind me. I turn to look at him. "Sorry. What?"

His face softens. "Lucy, if I might, you've been really off today. Something bothering you?"

I shake my head. "It's nothing. I'm sorry. I didn't sleep well last night."

He makes a low growl sound. "Like I tell these boys every

day, Lucy, I'm a fixer. Something's wrong with someone on my team, and that includes my coaching team, and I want to hear about it and I want to help fix it."

I blink away a tear and shake my head. "It's something personal. But it'll all be taken care of tomorrow." I remember that I have to be in court at nine. "I'm...I'm sorry but I'll have to miss the morning training session. I can send the plans to you and your assistants. Oh, god, the day before playoffs. Todd, I'm so sorry. But I have another commitment that I simply cannot reschedule."

"Hey," he rushes over and sets a thick hand on my arm. "Lucy, it's okay. We've got this. Didn't you say they'll be peaking tomorrow? You've got them well trained, honey. The men will be fine."

I look up to mutter some sort of thanks or an additional excuse but I see Hawk standing in my doorway behind Todd. His face is etched with concern. "Everything okay in here?"

I close my eyes and shake my head. "Todd was just checking in." I wipe my eyes with the heels of my hands. "I was explaining that I won't be at training tomorrow morning. Please extend my apologies to the rest of the team, Hawk."

Hawk and Coach exchange a glance and I fumble with the dry erase marker in my hand. Todd squints his eyes and looks at Hawk. He says, to me, "Look, Lucy, I know you and Moyer have struck up a friendship. I'm going to trust that you'll tell him what's eating at you and he will in turn tell me if it's something I need to know." He pats Hawk on the arm and Hawk nods solemnly. Coach walks out of my office and shuts the door behind him.

Hawk crosses his arms over his chest and leans against my desk. "Lucy, what's going on? You're white as a sheet."

I take a shuddering breath and tell him about court tomorrow, what Nick is trying to do, that Erika seems glad it's happening quickly and not something the judge is drawing out. Hawk nods, clenching his jaw. "I want to come with you to court," he says.

I gasp. "Hawk, no! It's during training." I shake my head rapidly. "Absolutely not. You cannot miss training for this. Erika says … just, no."

He flings his long arms out wide, taking up all the space in the room. "Jesus Christ, Lucy, will you never, ever let me be there for you? Come the fuck on! You have to be in the same room as this monster and you think I'm going to miss that?"

I clench my teeth together. "Yes, Hawk, I do. Because you and I are not allowed to be together and because you are a professional athlete starting in a playoff game the following morning. And your performance on the field will help determine whether I keep this job and can pay rent in a better, safer home for me and my son."

As I rant he steps closer to me. His face softens and he wraps his arms around me. "Okay, honey. I hear you." I gasp. He tips my chin up with a gentle finger. "I hear you. But I'm sending my brothers to be there in my place."

"What?"

He nods. "I'm sending my brothers. And they're going to watch out for you for me. And they're just going to be there in the hallway in case you encounter him and they're going to make a human Stag fucking shield and if they need to, they're going to ram their antlers into Nick's eyeballs for me."

I can't help but laugh. "Did you say antlers?"

He smiles. "I'm still workshopping jokes about my brothers." He pulls me into his arms and holds me until I actually do feel a little better.

When he leaves, the adrenaline returns. There's no denying it: I am not okay. I am far from okay. I sit at my desk and close my eyes. I focus on my breathing, and it helps a little. But not enough.

I have to figure out what to do. I can't go pick up Wyatt panicking like this. I can't drive to my apartment to get nice things for court when I'm frightened like this. I can't do anything right now. Not a damn thing! I feel helpless like I haven't felt in a long time and before I know it, I'm sitting on the floor with my back against the wall, gasping for breath.

Time passes. I swallow and remember the support group I attended at the women's center. The women there described similar waves of panic leading up to facing their abusers in court.

This is a normal response. I breathe slowly, like I coach the players to do when we're cooling down. I think about the meeting, the women all curling their hands into tight fists like I had. Like I'm doing right now. I loosen my fingers. I think to what I tell the Forge players and I shake my shoulders, rolling them to loosen them a bit. My muscles relax.

I think back to the support meeting, trying to focus on my breathing while I remember what I learned there. The facilitator suggested bringing someone along to court, someone to be there in support—of me. The center offers advocates who do this, but I bite my lip, hesitating at the thought of a stranger being with me for such a thing.

I'll have Patty with me tomorrow. Patty will be a strong, calming presence for sure. I remember that Hawk said his brothers will come to court. Tim is someone else who knows me, knows what's going on. I will have people there with me. I don't have to shoulder this alone. I am safe.

"I am safe," I say again. I realize I have a few different people I could call right now, and they'd listen. And I've worked really hard to build those relationships. I start to cry, but this time it's tears of relief. I stand up from the floor feeling better, feeling like maybe things are going to be okay.

CHAPTER THIRTY-FOUR
Lucy

Patty meets me outside the courthouse in the morning after I drop Wyatt at daycare. I had to leave our hotel extra early to swing by my apartment and get dressy clothes to wear to court. I grin, thinking Patty looks dapper in a suit, especially compared to the khakis and button down that will have to do for my outfit.

Patty hands me a coffee and smiles. "Hey, Lucy. How you feeling about today?"

I draw in a deep, shaky breath. "A lot of feelings, Professor. Nervous. Angry. Anxious." I tick the emotions off on my fingers and decide my hands are better off wrapped around the coffee cup. I drink gratefully as we walk inside.

"Well," Patty says, holding the door for me as we make our way to the security checkpoint. "I'm eager to share my view of what happened. I'm on team Lucy and Wyatt. But you already knew that, right?" She nudges me with her shoulder. I nod and set my purse on the metal detector. Once we're through, I'm not sure where to go.

Criminal cases all take place in a different building from the family court so I've never actually been in this courthouse before. Patty seems to know where to go and I'm grateful for her strong, friendly presence at my side. When we get to the floor of our courtroom, I gasp when I see a trio of suited men sitting on the benches in the hall.

Tim Stag and, I assume, his brothers stand when I approach. I tear up, realizing that Hawk really did call his brothers and ask them to be here in support since he wasn't able to miss training. Tim walks toward me and smiles. "Lucy, good to see you again. Although I'm sorry about the circumstances."

I shake his hand. "Hi, Tim. Thank you for being here. And…" I turn to his brothers. "Thank you. I don't know what to say."

The tall one grins and the bearded one sets his jaw. Tim places a hand on my shoulder. "I would have wanted to be here in support as legal counsel for the team even if my brother hadn't asked us to come look after you, Lucy."

Since the D.A. is the one prosecuting the criminal charges, Erika doesn't need to be here today and I was happy enough not to pay for her time. I'm about to tell Tim it really doesn't seem necessary for anyone to look after me, but then I see Nick walking in with, I assume, his lawyer. And his parents are right behind him. My knees almost buckle at the sight of him and I realize I am far from free of the trauma he inflicted on me. I'm grateful for the team I've got with me. They're just here for *me.*

Tim puts a supportive hand under my elbow and Patty presses in closer at my side. I clear my throat. "Tim, Stag brothers, this is my friend Patty." I blink away tears. "She's the one who saved Wyatt when Nick locked him in a stifling car while he went out drinking."

My voice is steady as I say that last part, and I know his parents can hear me. Part of me wishes Wyatt was here so they could see the impact their adult son had on his own child. But ultimately I'm glad he is spared seeing me visibly upset about this whole thing.

The prosecutor arrives from the district attorney's office and ushers Patty and me inside. Tim and his brothers sit in the row directly behind me. Every time Nick's lawyer stands up to speak, one of the Stag brothers places a reassuring hand on my shoulder. The beginning of the proceedings pass in a blur until Patty steps up to speak with the judge.

Nick's lawyer frames everything as if Patty was some sort of criminal, talking about how she vandalized his vehicle. Patty actually laughs at that language. "If that's how you want to word it, feel free," she says. "Yes. I shattered the vehicle window in an effort to save a terrified child from a sweltering car." Her eyes flash as she relays what happened and I anxiously shred tissues in my lap as I remember how hot it was that day, how easily my son could have died.

Patty eventually returns to my side and Tim leans forward. "You doing okay, Lucy? We can ask for a recess if you need." I shake my head rapidly. The judge is reviewing notes.

He stares at me and then shifts his gaze to Nick. "Can someone tell me why we're here today?"

Nick's lawyer starts to say something about the motion to suppress the charges, given the vandalism and the lack of Wyatt coming to harm, but the judge holds up a hand. "What I mean is, why am I being forced to endure this nonsense? Are you seriously suggesting I take seriously a motion to suppress these charges?"

The lawyer adjusts his tie. "Your honor, given the damage to Mr. DeLuca's vehicle, which the witness admitted to causing—"

"Enough with that." The judge looks irate. "I'm not suppressing the charges. I've heard enough of that. And for that matter, I want to know why in the holy hell the conditions of bail are not being met."

"Conditions, sir?"

The judge picks up a sheet of pink paper and I recognize it as coming from Erika. She must have been helping the D.A. put together pertinent information. The judge says, "Why am I looking at a report that the defendant followed this woman to her place of work and to her—" He squints at Nick and shakes his head. "Are you following her to soccer practice? Soccer practice? In the park?"

Nick's lawyer clears his throat. "Your honor, those issues are related to Mr. DeLuca's custody concerns."

"Enough. Enough." The judge presses his palms against the bench and leans into the microphone. He looks at Nick. "Do you want to go to jail?"

Nick shakes his head. "No, sir."

"Listen to me very carefully. These charges are going to stand. I want to be very clear that this no-contact order is going to stand. You are to have *no contact* with Ms. Nelson or with your son. If you look at them wrong, if you pick up the phone and call them, if you go on social media and poke them on Facebook, whatever it is. I will put you in jail so fast your head is gonna spin. Is that clear?"

Patty squeezes my hand as Nick fumbles to respond. "Yes, sir."

"You do not leave your house apart from work. I see that you have no driver's license because you haven't paid your child support in months, so you get yourself caught up with that, too." The judge points a finger at Nick's lawyer. "You've had long enough to deal with the psychiatric evaluation. Enough dawdling about that. I want it on my desk in a month."

The judge leans back in his chair shaking his head. "Do you understand my orders here?"

Nick clears his throat. "Those are very strict orders, sir."

I hear Tim gasp behind me and the D.A. starts laughing silently beside me. The judge's face turns bright red. "Strict? Son, you don't know from strict. I've had enough of this. I will see you at trial." He bangs his gavel and strides out of the room.

I look between Patty and the assistant district attorney. "So what just happened here?"

The D.A. raises his brows and says, "He's about to burn in

a fire of his own making."

Tim squeezes my shoulder again. "Your ex pissed off the judge and his lawyer's attempt to get rid of the charges blew up in his face. You and Wyatt are a lot closer to being safe, Lucy."

"Really?" I choke back tears and wrap my arms around Patty. "I don't know how to thank you." I step back and gesture to Tim and his brothers. "All of you."

"Lucy, you don't need to thank us." Tim takes my hand now, patting it. His brothers nod.

"I wouldn't say no to VIP seats at the Forge game tomorrow." Patty winks. "But seriously, Lucy. I did what I would want anyone to do for me or for my daughters."

Hawk's bearded brother grunts approvingly at Patty. The tall Stag leans down and grins. "I'm here because my brother cares about you, and that means I care about you. But I wouldn't say no to some sweet soccer seats, if you can make that happen." Tim smacks him in the chest. "What? Our brother has a playoff game tomorrow."

I laugh, finally feeling lighter. "I'll get tickets for all of you.   I   promise."

CHAPTER THIRTY-FIVE

Hawk

Complete Stag Brothers Group Chat

Ty: The eagle has left the building.

Thatcher: I told u not to use a code name for Lucy, Ty.

Tim: What Ty means to say is that court went well and we're bringing Lucy to the stadium. She's getting her car from the garage right now.

Me: Seriously? That didn't take long.

Tim: That's because he had no case and only succeeded in pissing off the judge. Ty, remind me to give Juniper the run-down later.

Ty: Dude, I'm standing right next to you.

Tim: I'm documenting for posterity.

I kept my phone in my pocket for the first hour of training, super anxious about what was going on with Lucy. Coach asked me again this morning if there was anything he needed to know about her missing work this morning and I told him I'd update him later.

I jog over to him on the sideline after I hear from my brothers. "Coach," I try to draw him away from the assistants and I'm glad when he understands and steps toward me. "I just wanted to let you know Lucy's on her way here and I think things are going to be okay."

My brother Tim wouldn't exaggerate or misrepresent what happened. Coach grins at this news. "Glad to hear that, Moyer. Good."

I hand him my phone. "Hold that for me?"

He shakes his head. "Christ, kid. You've been running sprints with this thing on you?" I shrug. "Get back out there, Moyer."

Lucy arrives in between training and film, and she smiles at me, but I don't get a chance to talk to her. I pop into her office when we're done for the day, but she's hustling down the hallway. "I have to get Wyatt," she says. She bites her lip. "We have to check out of our hotel."

I arch a brow at her. "Hotel? You've been paying for a hotel? Since when?"

She shakes her head. "It doesn't matter." She pauses for an instant, like she's trying to decide something huge. "Do you want to come with me? We can talk in the car?"

"Of course I want to come with you, Lucy." I shake my head and follow her and I take her bag from her as she unlocks her trunk, dropping her stuff and mine into the space full of her son's toys. I buckle my seatbelt as she drives toward Wyatt's daycare and she tells me about court.

"I feel like someone finally heard me," she says, eyes on the road. Like it's easier for her to open up without looking at me. I'll take it. "I know it's terrible, but that was one of the thoughts I had the night Nick locked Wyatt in that car. That someone saw now, that it wasn't all inside my head. That he actually is a dangerous person."

I frown. "What's stopping him from just following you again, coming after you two? He's still on house arrest?"

She nods. "The same mechanisms as before, but now he and his parents and his lawyer know that they're actually monitoring him. That they are serious. I wish you could have seen the judge, Hawk. He hates Nick." Lucy allows herself a grin at this revelation.

"I wish I could have been there, too, but someone insisted I stay with the team and finish her last brutal workout before playoffs…"

She swats at my arm. "Your brothers were really amazing. I really like them, Hawk."

I laugh. "I like them, too. Not that I have a choice about it."

She tells me how Tim debriefed her with his opinion afterward and how they called Juniper, who confirmed that the judge indeed does not mess around with idle threats. "If he said he'd toss Nick in jail for his behavior, Juniper says he's really serious about it and it doesn't matter how much money Nick's family has to throw at appeals."

"I'm glad she's able to give us the inside scoop."

Lucy grins. "Speaking of your family, I promised them all VIP seats at the match tomorrow."

My stomach flutters at this idea, that my brothers and their wives and children will come watch me play. "My mom will be there, too," I tell her, and then I realize that my mom is going to meet my brothers, come face to face with the children of the man she feared for 26 years.

Lucy pats my arm as she pulls into the parking spot outside Wyatt's daycare. "Speaking as a mother," she says, "I'm sure she will have a lot of big feelings, but the main thing will be that she sees you happy with them, that they care about you, too."

Lucy and Wyatt drop me outside my apartment so I can eat my prescribed dinner and get the recommended amount of sleep before our playoff game. I don't get a chance to talk to my mom or my brothers in the morning before I head to the stadium for the afternoon match.

I draw on my years of training to get ready for the game, telling myself there will be plenty of time to fuss over my family later. I silence the excited surge I feel at the idea of introducing my mother to Lucy. So much is still up in the air between us, but I'm not willing to ease up. Not when we've been through so much together. Not when I have such big plans to make sure she knows she can have anything she wants. And I know she wants me. I know it.

The team is pumped to play against Atlanta. Everyone is literally jumping up and down as we take the field before the match. We had an amazing final run through together, and all of us are fit. We've had a long run with no injuries and our starting lineup is the same crew who dominated New York. I'm not worried about the game.

My eyes keep wandering up to the box, where I know my mother is sitting in a row of seats with my brothers. Where Lucy's son is running around with my boss's kids. I shake my head and my arms, telling my body to focus. I've got 90 minutes of work to do before I can worry about all of that.

We win 2-1 with a late goal from Reggie, who is still screaming joyfully in the showers. Coach urges him to hurry his ass up, since the media is waiting to interview him for a change. I'm glad of the reprieve from attention. I hurry through my own shower so I can find my family. When I make my way up to the VIP box, where I asked everyone to wait, I'm bombarded by a tangle of long limbs.

My brothers squeeze me into their arms, soon joined by my nine nephews, all jumping up and down and wearing Moyer jerseys, squealing. I feel like I'm being squeezed by a red and black striped raccoon. Over Tim's shoulder, I see my mom, deep in conversation with Lucy's friend Patty. The two of them have their heads bent together over a cellphone, laughing.

I extract myself from the hug and grin. Ty ruffles my hair. "That was a sweet assist you had there, bruh."

"Bruh?" Thatcher arches a brow as he scoops up one of the kids. Byron I think? But before I can delve deeper into the

Stag family tree, my mom catches my eye and rushes over to squeeze me in another series of deep hugs.

"Hey, Ma," I say, scooping her into the air and twirling her around. I set her on the ground and she wipes away tears, smiling. I scratch my neck and look around the box. "So…you met my brothers?"

She nods and the three of them smile at her, more subdued. "I did," she says. She clasps her hands together in front of her heart. "Oh, Hawk, I'm so happy for you, honey."

CHAPTER THIRTY-SIX
Lucy

Monday comes with a flurry of excitement. The Forge will play in the championship this coming weekend against L.A. That means we have to balance media appearances with their final week of training, watching film, medical checkups and meetings about endorsement deals that have come flooding in for a lot of the players.

Today, the team set the press conference first thing and I'll be leading the team through their workout soon after. With nothing else pressing to do, I decide to head into the media room to watch as Hawk, Todd and Jacques speak to the press. I'm glad to see Reggie in there as well. He deserves some more of the spotlight after that game-winning goal he had on Saturday.

I smile, remembering how much his stats have improved since I started helping the team train.

The media outlets begin with their typical round of questions about the upcoming game and how the guys are feeling about their chances, their teamwork, and L.A.'s starting striker who joined the team from Brazil.

But then the questions turn to what the team has planned for after the season, when many of the players focus on their charity work and various endorsements. Reggie and Jacques talk about returning to their hometowns in Canada, where they'll be coaching youth programs over the winter.

A hush falls over the room when the cameras turn to Hawk, who seems to have a statement prepared. I lean forward in my seat, curious. He didn't mention anything about this Saturday night or Sunday, when he spent the day watching movies with Wyatt and me at our apartment.

I thought he'd be hanging out with his brothers all weekend, but no. He said he wanted to watch *Toy Story* and play Legos. And he didn't ask me anything about Nick, didn't press me to talk about my feelings. He was just...there. Present.

Hawk clears his throat. "Thank you for this question. It means a lot to me. As I've said before, I was raised by a single mother who didn't always have the easiest time providing a safe home for me."

"Hawk, were you the anonymous donor who gave a million dollars to the housing fund in Loudonville?" A reporter stands and barks out the question from the middle of the room. Hawk turns his gaze to the reporter.

"I'll be happy to take questions in a few minutes. I want to say something, though." The reporter sits back down, cheeks flushed as the rest of the reporters glare at him. I chuckle, until Hawk starts talking again.

"A lot of women struggle to keep their kids safe, and a big barrier to that is the high cost of quality legal support. I'm excited to announce that I've joined the board of the Women's Legal Support foundation in Pittsburgh." A hush falls over the room and I feel my heart surge in my chest. I swallow down a bunch of emotions I'm not ready for as Hawk continues talking. "Along with a sizable financial contribution, I'm offering my connections to the foundation, to help spread the word about the good work they do, and about how men who really care about keeping women safe...can do so."

The reporters all start to murmur and Kioko beams at

Hawk, stepping behind him to pat him on the back. "So yeah. That's how I'll be spending the off season." He pauses and leans into the mic again. "Oh, and yes, I contributed to an organization in my hometown that supported my mother when I was a baby."

There's a loaded silence in the room and then a female reporter stands up, applauding with her notebook tucked under one arm. Hawk's teammates at the front table applaud as well and soon the room erupts with excited questions. It all becomes a blur for me, though, as I try to process what's happening. This man who has for months been telling me he cares, has gone out and shown me how much he means it. I can hardly form words, thinking about how his contribution will help so many women like me, who just need a little bit of support in order to be free.

Hawk fields questions as I stare at him, my fingers clutching the seat in front of me, my heart soaring. He went and threw money at a problem that matters to me. And he's giving his time and his face to the cause. I feel a strong urge to run up to him and rip his clothes off.

Eventually the room empties out, mostly. Todd gives me a salute as he walks past on his way to his office, but Hawk stops in front of my seat.

I stand up, tears sliding down my face. "Hey," he says.

I open my mouth to respond, but no words come out. Instead, I leap toward his body, his arms wrapping around me in surprise as I kiss him and try to convey my gratitude that way since words have failed me.

"Lucy," he breathes into my mouth.

"Hawk, this is everything," I say between kisses. "Everything."

"I did it for you. In honor of you, and your strength," he says, causing another sob to sneak out of my throat.

And then I notice Kioko standing in the doorway, concern clouding his typical smile. He clears his throat. Hawk steps backward and runs a hand through his hair.

Kioko crosses his arms over his chest. "May I see you both in my office, please?"

We walk up to Kioko's office and don't speak as we wait for him to join us. A few minutes later, he enters the room with Tim Stag and the lawyer who took over managing Forge business after it was revealed that Tim and Hawk are brothers. I'm relieved to see Tim here today. I've come to think of him as a safe and calming person.

Kiko gestures not to the couch, but to the more official table at the back of the room, and we all slip into the chairs as I fight the urge to grab Hawk's hand.

Tim clears his throat. "It's come to our attention that a physical relationship has developed between a member of the coaching staff and a player on the Pittsburgh Forge," he says. He gestures to his colleague. "I happened to begin a review of the Forge employee handbook recently." He catches Hawk's eye and I notice a small nod between the brothers. "There is currently no policy in place at all about this sort of relationship and, thus, no policy has been broken."

Kioko's eyebrows raise and his face relaxes a few degrees. "Is that so?" He directs this question to Tim's colleague, who nods rapidly.

Tim continues talking. "Many organizations have policies in place about romantic relationships between management staff and their subordinates, but the world of professional sports seems to be remiss in establishing these sorts of policies. I know this because my firm, as you know, manages many different types of sports teams." Tim adjusts his tie and explains his assumption that nobody ever stopped to think women might step into these sorts of leadership roles or that same-sex relationships would ever emerge between players and staff. He shrugs. "My former colleague Juniper Jones reminded me that there are a number of Olympic track and swimming athletes married to their coaches. There's precedent, in other words, for these relationships to exist among successful competition."

I stare at Tim and turn my head to Hawk, who doesn't seem shocked about any of this. I start to wonder how much Tim knew about this in advance, whether Hawk confided in his brother or sought advice beforehand. But I'm the one who dove into his arms and kissed him at work.

Kioko scratches his chin. "I cannot abide any additional scandal," he says. "I'm still reeling from the incident last season." Tim nods. "But also, this season…this season has been nothing short of spectacular." Hawk grins. Kioko points a finger at me. "Since you have joined us, you and Hawk both, we have soared to new heights. We have become a team to be reckoned with. That is something special."

I nod my head, still too stunned to speak. Today has been filled with highs and lows, an emotional roller coaster. Kioko turns to Tim and his staffer. "What is your legal advice in this regard?"

Tim clears his throat again and opens a folder. His colleague smiles. "As I mentioned, I happened to be looking into the employee handbook prior to this event. And I'm not serving the Forge in an official capacity since my brother is a player and I lack objectivity." Everyone around the table nods. Tim continues. "I recommend this policy, which requires anyone entering a romantic relationship to disclose said relationship to a member of management, who will keep the information discreet."

The room is silent as everyone considers this and I find it hard to believe things could really be this easy, that it might not actually be a disqualifying factor if I continue to pursue things with Hawk. My mouth hangs open as I look around the table.

Kioko leans toward me and asks, "Lucy, is there anything you wish to disclose at this time?"

Hawk grins and squeezes my leg under the table. I jump. "Um, yes?" Kioko nods and gestures for me to continue. "I, um, would like to disclose a…relationship with one of the players, sir."

He smiles. "Is that so? And which player would this be?"

I tuck my hair behind my ears and smile. "It's Hawk. Hawk Moyer." I nod and stare at him. "I'd very much like to continue to pursue a romantic relationship."

CHAPTER THIRTY-SEVEN
Hawk

The Forge lose to L.A. 3-1. I should be more upset after the final whistle. I should be devastated to lose in the championship match. But none of us are. Nobody expected us to make it here, not this year. To come second place in the entire league, our first year playing at this level? I'm pretty damn proud, actually.

And looking around the field, at the rest of the guys with smiles on their faces, I think the feeling is mutual. A few weeks ago I wouldn't have necessarily imagined feeling like hugging them all. I was too busy being angry about my family history, and it clouded my vision until I almost missed some really good things standing right in front of me.

Hell, yesterday when we had a team meeting to disclose my relationship with Lucy, I was really worried the guys would feel irritated or worry about the starting lineup. But everyone seemed to take it in stride. It definitely didn't impact our play today. We were really in sync and I think every one of us knows we gave it our all.

After we're done slapping hands and listening to Coach talk about how proud he is of our progress and how much he's looking forward to settling unfinished business next season, I'm itching to finish some personal business I've been working very hard on lately.

I bypass the locker room and climb up the bleachers toward the VIP box, in search of Lucy. Actually, I'm not really looking for Lucy in this exact moment. I'm trying to find Wyatt and I'm hoping I made it up here before his mom came up to grab him. There's something really important I need to ask my little buddy.

I reach the box and wave at Tawnya, who grins when she sees me and points toward a long table, where a set of twin girls is deeply involved with some sort of hand slapping game with Tawnya's twin boys. Wyatt sits beside them, cheering.

I do a double take for a minute when I see my mom in a romantic embrace with Lucy's friend Patty. I remember that the twin girls are Patty's daughters, but I wasn't expecting to see my mother today at all, let alone nuzzling with my girlfriend's teammate.

Girlfriend. Right. "Hey, Wyatt," I say, crouching down next to him. "Can I ask you something?"

"Hawk Moyerrrrr," he says, grinning like usual. "What?"

I gesture for him to follow me to a group of seats overlooking the pitch, which is still abuzz with grounds crew and media cameras and fans lingering long after the whistle. "Wyatt, I wondered what you'd think if I took your mom on a date."

"A date? Like for ice cream?"

I shrug. "Sure. Ice cream, movies, that kind of thing."

He scrunches up his face. "Would there be sprinkles again?"

I grin. "If your mom wants sprinkles, sure."

He seems to consider and then shrugs. "Yep. That would be fine."

"Yeah? I want to make sure it's okay with you, since I know you're the main man in your mom's life." I look above him when I see a shadow and Lucy is standing there, tears in her eyes, a surprised expression on her face. She's been crying a lot this week, but it seems like the happy kind of tears.

"Yep. Can I go back and play with the twins now?"

I nod and he dashes away, giving Lucy a quick squeeze as he rushes to get back to the game.

"Did you just ask my son his permission to date me?" She puts her hands on her hips and stands above me.

I ease out of the chair and nod. "Sure did. Thought I'd seek his opinion before he walks in on me ravishing you."

She spits out a laugh. "Hawk, he's not going to walk in."

"That's what you think," I say, pulling her into my arms and smiling down at her. "But you only have one room for now, and you're nuts if you think I'm not spending every night with you from now on."

She raises one eyebrow and squints at me. "Every night, huh?"

I   nod.   "Every   single   one."

CHAPTER THIRTY-EIGHT

Lucy

Hawk's idea of a hot date is apparently to come watch me play soccer with the Phe-Moms. Since it's the off-season, he volunteers to pick Wyatt up from daycare for me and by the time I'm done putting up my hair and changing into my soccer stuff, the two of them are standing in the living room wearing matching shirts that say "Phe-MOM-enal."

"Where'd you guys get those?" I laugh, scooping Wyatt up to kiss him.

Hawk grins and shrugs. "Had them made special. I've got some for Kioko and his kids, too."

Wyatt starts jumping up and down. "Can I give them to Natori and Odongo?"

Hawk ruffles his hair as we walk out to climb into my car. "Sure, pal."

When we get to the field, Hawk takes my hand as we climb the hill to the turf. I hesitate at first, still unused to just being with him, physically, publicly. But he gives a reassuring squeeze as Wyatt sprints ahead of us.

I drop my bag on the sideline and grin as some of the Phe-Moms come to check out Hawk's shirt, and then they recognize him. Tawnya bursts into a grin and jogs over to us. "Um, you two are super cute right now." She puts her hand on her hip and squints at Hawk. "I hope you're here to chase down balls for us when someone kicks out of bounds."

He grins. "Obviously."

We stretch and the game starts. Every few plays, I hear Hawk whistle and clap his hands, cheering for everyone each time a Phe-Mom player does something exciting. "Nice pass," he hollers repeatedly. "Amazing defense!"

We stop for a water break and he massages my shoulders. Patty smiles and gives me a thumbs up. For the rest of the evening, Hawk cheers for our pick-up game as if he were watching a professional championship soccer match. Every time someone sends a ball out of bounds, he sprints into the trees to grab it for us. Tawnya points at me. "I could get used to you bringing him around, Lucy." There's a chorus of agreement from the other players and I flush.

After the game, I see Hawk whispering with Tawnya and Wyatt jumping up and down with the twins. She smiles and gives me a thumbs up and I walk over to them, curious. Hawk drapes an arm around my shoulders, and I realize it doesn't feel manipulative or possessive at all. It just feels nice. I snuggle up against his side as he says, "Wyatt is going to have a sleepover at Tawnya's house. I'll grab him in the morning and take him to daycare *and* I'll bring takeout pancakes for everyone."

My eyebrows shoot up and I open my mouth to protest, instinctively worrying that I'm taking advantage of my friend's kindness. But she actually places a hand over my mouth. "Nope. Not gonna listen to you try to say no. It was my idea."

Hawk laughs. "Hello? I'm trying to do a grand gesture here? Can't it be my idea?"

"Nope!" Tawnya laughs. "I never want Lucy to forget that I'm the friend who enabled her to have a hot evening alone with her sexy soccer player." She leans in close so the kids can't hear us. "As soon as you get a new place I promise to let you reciprocate." She winks and turns to grab the kids, heading to her car.

I stand under the lights staring up at Hawk's smile. "This is already the best date I've had in a while."

He arches a brow. "In a while? When was the last good one?"

I grin. "When I almost prevented you from scoring at the Forge field."

"Oh, really?" He reaches into my bag and grabs my ball and grins, yanking my duffel from me and dropping it on the turf. "I bet you still can't score on me, Lucy."

He sprints toward the field the Phe-Moms just vacated, dribbling the ball between his sneakers as he runs away from me toward the goal. He turns and jogs backward away from the ball, beckoning toward me with his hand. I laugh and run onto the field, volleying possession of the ball back and forth a few times before he finally draws it back with his toe and fakes around me, sprinting down the field and scoring in the opposite net. He meets me in the center of the field, both of us breathing heavy, smiling.

"I win again," he says.

"Still cocky," I retort.

"God, I love when you mispronounce my name." He bends to kiss me and scoops me into his arms, carrying me toward the car. He climbs into the drivers seat and speeds toward his apartment, his hand roaming over my thigh, driving me crazy as he drives a little recklessly.

We pass his neighbors in the hall and they look like they're about to talk to him, but he silences them by throwing me over his shoulder. I squeak out an apology and they laugh as Hawk unlocks the door and runs down the hall to his bedroom. "I get you all to myself til morning, Lucy the Milf," he growls, peeling off my clothes and licking my stomach. He laughs. "You're very salty."

"Well I just played a lot of soccer," I tell him, my hand trailing through his dark hair. "I'm pretty dirty."

"Mmm, I can make you dirty," he says, laughing as he peels my sports bra up and over my head. I'm bare for him, lying on his bed in the moonlight. He kneels over me and traces a finger down my body. "Lucy, you're so beautiful."

I smile and reach for his shoulder, pulling him to me, savoring the weight of him on top of me. I love how I feel pressed into the mattress, so safe and secure with him. I can feel his devotion through every kiss, hear his feelings through every moan and whisper of my name. When he's naked and hard and pulsing in my hand, he says, "Lucy, I want to feel you, just us with no barriers."

I look up at him, knowing this is a very big deal for him. I swallow. "Are you sure, Hawk? I still have the implant, so I can't get pregnant."

"I trust you," he breathes, his words hot against my lips. "I trust you."

"I trust you, too," I gasp, using my hand to line him up and ease the tip of him, already weeping precum inside me. He's so hot and smooth, the feeling electric as he slides inside. We both groan at the sensation of our joining, bare and as close as it's possible for us to be.

I think of all the ways he pushed me to see how much he cares about me, all the ways he showed me he wants to create a safe world for me and for my son. As he thrusts inside me I think about how much he respects the work I do when it comes to his fitness, his endurance.

"I love you," I say as I realize it.

"God, Lucy, I love you, too." He rests his forehead against mine, his hands on the mattress by my head as he thrusts slowly inside me. I feel his heart beating against mine and I swear our pulses synch up as we move together.

And then I stop analyzing and give in to the sensations as his fingers find my nipples, his teeth nip at my ear lobes. His long, thick fingers find my clit and he brings me up and over the cliff of ecstasy. Somewhere along the way, he joins me and I can feel him pouring his pleasure inside me. My body throbs around his and I hold him tight against me, never wanting to let him go.

I wake up tangled in Hawk, in his sheets and his limbs and his scent. I remember I never did shower after practice and I groan, reaching for my phone to turn off the alarm. I realize the alarm is coming from Hawk's phone, since mine isn't set. I don't have a job to wake up for...unless...

Hawk kisses my neck and squints at the glare from my screen in the morning darkness. "Whatcha doing, Lucy?"

I hold my breath, seeing a notification that I have a new email in my work account. Is it still my work account? Hawk looks over my shoulder as I open the message, seeing the subject line "Contract of Employment."

I gasp and I feel his arms tighten around my waist. I read the message, from Kioko, until I get to the phrase, "we are delighted to offer you full-time, permanent employment."

"I knew it," Hawk cries and a nervous laugh escapes me. I realize I've been clenching my body for a long time now, well before I met Hawk Moyer. I look at the contract in my hand and think about all it promises. Financial security. Health insurance. My career goals.

"Is this real?" I ask him, and he nods, smiling wide. I hop out of bed and jump up and down, clapping my hands like Wyatt in my joy and excitement. "Everything is working out," I mutter, and then I sink to the bed as the emotion of it all catches up with me.

I'm well and truly free, and I'm thriving. My son and I are safe, I have my dream job and I have a man in my life who cares about me, supports me, celebrates my success. I turn my head and through my tears I see him smiling at me, his hand on my knee supportively.

"I love you," I whisper. He pulls me in for a hug and kisses the top of my head again.

"I love you, too, babe. Also, you stink." He joins me in the shower and we use all the hot water, together.

EPILOGUE: HAWK

"You ready?" Lucy kisses me in the kitchen as I stare out the window of my apartment. Wyatt isn't up yet, the door to my second bedroom still closed and all is quiet. I pull her in and hug her, nuzzling my chin against the top of her head. I nod.

This morning, I'm running a turkey trot with my brothers before our Thanksgiving dinner at Tim and Alice's house. But that's not what I'm anxious about. After we run, they're taking me to Thatcher's house to meet our father.

"Deep breaths, babe," Lucy says, placing a hand on my chest. She breathes with me a few times and smiles. "I'm just a phone call away if you need me."

I nod and she stretches up on tiptoe to kiss my forehead before walking back into the bedroom. Despite the off season, she's been working long hours with Todd and the coaching staff making plans for the fall, sending out workouts to each of the players and getting situated in her new apartment two floors above mine.

She and Wyatt moved in a few weeks ago, but they both spend most of their nights at my house. I'm not complaining. It makes Lucy feel secure knowing she has her own space to retreat to. I thought it would be nice having an extra space for my mom to stay when she comes to town…but she's been dating Lucy's friend Patty and decided to stay with her for Thanksgiving. It was strange watching the Phe-Moms last night with my mom, both of us cheering for our girlfriends. But it's also kind of nice having our own cheering section.

I take a deep breath and head out, stopping at Thatcher's

to grab him before driving to the 5k start line, where Tim and Ty are waiting for us. We're quiet throughout the race, which shows me how much they're all feeling the weight of this, too. And then I get nervous, wondering if I should call Lucy or my mom or just call the whole thing off altogether.

"Hey," Thatcher says, looking over at me. "You got this. We'll all be there." Thatcher tells me how Ted has started going to more meetings since he found out about me so he didn't relapse. He also started volunteering with the women's shelter, helping out with some of the sobriety programs that helped my mom when she was pregnant with me. He's trying to live a better life and I feel ready to meet him where he is.

I nod a few times and pull into his carport, raking my hands through my hair and taking a deep breath. I look out the window where Ty and Tim are pulling up to the house, waiting for me at the door before heading upstairs. Thatcher lives in an industrial loft and we have to take an elevator to get up there. His house has one of those sliding doors that take forever to open and I feel a lump in my throat waiting for the glimpse of my father.

Thatcher pokes his head inside to look and then beckons for us to come in. I stand in the doorway, frozen in place as my brothers walk in and stand in a sort of semicircle around a graying, slender man with tears running down his face. "Hawk," he croaks, before covering his face with his hands and sobbing into his fingers.

I feel a surge of emotions and a lump in my throat, which I clear, and say, "Ted."

He seems to gather himself together and takes a step toward me, looking me up and down. I see a lot of myself in his face, in his build. His eyes are ringed by dark circles and his hands shake as he reaches for me. I reach out my hand and shake his. "I've wanted to meet you my whole life," I say.

He takes a deep, shaking breath and says, "I wish I knew about you sooner." I nod and I hear my brothers cough to cover up a wave of emotions I know they're all feeling.

"You look like me," I say, which is stupid and unnecessary because I obviously look like all my brothers. But the comment draws a smile.

"All my boys look alike," he says, gesturing around the room.

After a few minutes of silence, Ty claps our father on the back. "We all have similar appetites, too," Ty says. "Grab your coat, Ted. It's time for Thanksgiving."

The five of us squeeze into Ty's minivan after tossing a mountain of booster seats into the trunk area. I sit in the second row with our father, and the two of us stare at each other for most of the ride. Lucy insists things will get easier as time goes on, that we will think of the right things to say to one another. I know she's right.

Ty looks at me in the rearview mirror. "You know," he says, "the three of us OG Stag kids all have the same ink." Thatcher turns to look at him. Thatcher is heavily tattooed, and I know Ty doesn't mean they all have all the same tattoos.

"Oh yeah? What of?"

"It's a Stag," Tim says from the third row behind me. "Our wives have it, too."

"It's seriously so hot," Ty says, grinning. "Even June-bug got it, which got me thinking. She doesn't have our last name, but she's in the family."

"Obviously," I say, unsure where he's going with this.

Ted looks around the van at his sons. "I didn't know you boys all got a tattoo," he says. We approach a red light and Ty yanks down his t-shirt, revealing a leaping stag and laurel branches on his pec. Ted sucks in a breath. "Laurel," he says.

Thatcher nods. Ty looks at me in the rearview again. "Our mother. Laurel," he says, smiling. We pull onto Tim's street and I see the commotion of his home. The yard is full of Stag boys and I spy Wyatt running amidst the fray. A trio of women stands in the driveway keeping watch as the ten boys sprint up and down the sidewalk. Lucy is one of them, laughing and chatting with Juniper and Emma.

"Anyway," Ty says, "You should think about getting inked like us." He grins.

I look again at Lucy, whose face seems genuinely relaxed as she chats with my sisters-in-law. In a few short months of knowing her, she's transformed into someone with confidence and calm. She still has her moments of self-doubt, and I do, too.

But we remind each other that we both have networks now. We have people who care and our stories now include a whole herd of Stags who will stop at nothing to support us. She looks up and sees the van, her face brightening. She runs over to the sliding door and as soon as I open it, she's in my arms.

"I missed you," she says, kissing me. And then she draws back, biting her lip, her unspoken question written on her face. I swallow and reach for her hand, turning behind me to where my father is still trying to dislodge himself from the van.

"Ted," I say as he looks up. "I want you to meet Lucy, the

love of my life." She melts against my side and smiles at my father, waving. Wyatt runs over and wedges himself in between me and Lucy, clinging to both our legs.

My father smiles, his eyes tearing up yet again. "You have a beautiful family, Hawk," he says. He steps out of the van and stands in the driveway in the sunshine, surveying the hoard of people swarming around the house.

"Yeah." I pull Lucy in tight and kiss the top of her head. "Yeah, I do."

~~~

Thank you so much for reading the Stag brothers series!

Want to see more of these guys? They show up a lot in my Brady family series.

It all starts with **Foundation: A Grouchy Geek Romance**.

Want to see if Hawk gets the Stag family tattoo?

My newsletter subscribers get a bonus epilogue.

laineydavis.com

AUTHOR'S NOTE

Holy cow, I wrote another Stag brothers book! I never even imagined writing a Christmas special for this family, let alone a fifth book introducing an entirely new Stag. What happened was I got my COVID-19 booster and was in a fever haze for about 48 hours. During that haze, this book came to me, pretty much fully formed. A secret sibling!

I had so much fun putting this book together.

I want to give a particular nod to the women I've been playing soccer with this past year. Like Lucy, I joined a women's soccer team where everyone is over 30 and almost everyone is a mom. Talk about a lifesaver during pandemic! A few times a week, we meet up and play pickup soccer. That's it, but it's also so much more. I hoped to show how much a supportive network meant to Lucy, how the other women pushed her to tune out the noise in her life and focus on her game, even if it was just for that 90 minutes.

I also want to thank the many women in my life who have shared their stories with me as they have broken free of the clutches of a harmful intimate partner. I wish Nick, his actions, and his parents' actions were outlandish fiction. Unfortunately, he is a mashup of countless awful partners terrorizing women every day.

I had the wonderful opportunity this past year to meet some of the powerful women in the justice system, both behind the bench and working in defense of women and families. I am inspired by their work and hope my words pay tribute to their stories.

Thank you so much for reading Beautiful Game! Some day very soon, I'll start working on the stories of the next generation of Stag men. I hope you'll join me for the ride.

~Lainey

Printed in Great Britain
by Amazon